Dear Reader,

Welcome to Blackfoot Falls, Montana, home of the Sundance ranch and the rough-and-tumble McAllister clan. This is the first book in my Made in Montana series, which brings me back to the romantic world of the cowboy and the beauty of the American West.

I've always loved movies and books set in the West. Once in a while, Hollywood makes a Western and I'm first in line for a ticket. And I love making up my own stories, especially since I get to customize the heroes.

In *Barefoot Blue Jean Night,* you'll meet Cole McAllister, the eldest of three brothers—and definitely the strong silent type. To tell you the truth, I had trouble sharing him. I wanted to keep him for myself. But hopefully heroine Jamie Daniels and you all will appreciate him as much as I do.

Happy reading!

Debbi Rawlins

Debbi Rawlins

BAREFOOT BLUE JEAN NIGHT

HARLEQUIN®
entertain, enrich, inspire™

Recycling programs
for this product may
not exist in your area.

ISBN-13: 978-0-373-79705-9

BAREFOOT BLUE JEAN NIGHT

ABOUT THE AUTHOR

Debbi Rawlins lives in central Utah, out in the country, surrounded by woods and deer and wild turkeys. It's quite a change for a city girl who didn't even know where the state of Utah was until a few years ago. Of course, unfamiliarity has never stopped her. Between her junior and senior years of college, she spontaneously left her home in Hawaii and bummed around Europe for five weeks by herself. And much to her parents' delight, returned home with only a quarter in her wallet.

Books by Debbi Rawlins

This is for Laura Barth.
Thank you for your support, encouragement
and hard work.
You rock!

1

"Ease up, boy." Pulling on the reins of his horse, Cole McAllister squinted across a thousand acres of McAllister land at the late June sun sinking toward the soaring Rockies. He never wore a watch, didn't need to. The sun's position in the blue Montana sky told him he had just enough time to ride home and grab a shower before his sister arrived. The party would have already started, but he didn't care about missing any of the festivities. A quiet family dinner would have been his choice to celebrate Rachel's return after finishing graduate school.

He was excited to have his only sister back, equally pleased not to have to come up with more tuition money. The family ranch was officially operating on fumes. No one knew how desperately they needed cash but him. Both his brothers had some idea of the trouble they faced, Jesse more than Trace. After Jesse's two tours in Afghanistan, Cole got the feeling he didn't miss much.

Trace was still young, only twenty-six and most concerned with how soon he could trade in his pickup for a newer model. It wasn't that Cole had tried to hide anything—though the boys had agreed not to burden their mother or Rachel—but each month the economy just kept sliding further downhill, sinking them deeper into the hole.

Beef consumption was down, fuel and grain prices up. Any number of reasons accounted for their predicament, and they weren't alone. Most of the other ranches around Blackfoot Falls were in debt and disrepair, yet Cole still felt responsible. For six generations the Sundance had been passed from eldest son to eldest son and despite droughts and land disputes, recessions and wars, the McAllisters had survived on wits and grit. Cole would be damned if he'd be the first to go begging.

Bad enough that when some of the smaller ranches had started to buckle, men Cole had known his whole life had lost their jobs and come to him. Oh, he'd had work for them, but no means to pay them. That he had to turn them away about broke him in two. But it was all he could do to keep from laying off his own hands—some of them had hired on with his dad and were building fences and rounding up cattle before he was born.

They'd been there eleven years ago to console the family the day Cole's father had lost his final battle with cancer. They were the same men who'd loved and respected the formidable but fair Gavin McAllister as if he were their own kin, and they suffered his loss in the same way.

That hadn't stopped a single one of them from stepping in to give Cole a leg up in managing the three-thousand-acre cattle ranch. He'd turned twenty-one the week before, too young to fill his father's impressive boots. But it wasn't as if he'd had a choice. Even if he had, he wouldn't have changed anything. He'd been proud to pick up the reins, scared spitless but willing and honored. Who knew he'd bring the family to this?

He exhaled slowly, took a final long look at the land, dotted by the last vestiges of wildflowers—field daisies and pink columbine barely able to hang on this late in summer and only because of the altitude. The thought that they'd have to sell even a square foot of McAllister land twisted his gut in raw disgust that even his horse seemed to feel. Tango reared up. Cole tugged on the reins and leaned over to soothingly stroke the gelding's neck.

"Hey, buddy. Rachel's coming home today. You'll be happy to see her." He wheeled Tango around and since the horse had been watered and rested, Cole nudged him into a gallop. He took off, at one with the stiff, warm breeze.

They wove through the aspens until they broke out into the open meadow and raced across the tall thick grass, the sun fierce on Cole's back. He didn't slow them down until he saw a pair of veteran hands working along the fenceline, and he waved for them to return to the ranch so they could enjoy the barbecue. The crazy old fools would work till sundown if he didn't stop them. That's what made the situation so damn hard. Everyone from Chester, the bunkhouse cook, to the last hired wrangler took pride in the Sundance as if it were his own. If it came down to layoffs…

Cole could barely think in that direction. There would be no choice at that point. He'd have to auction off some of the land. Hell, what was he thinking? There'd be no auction. Wallace Gunderson would be the first one muddying up the McAllister porch, pen and checkbook in hand. Not only was he the sole person with that kind of money around here, but the old man had lusted after the hilly creek-fed McAllister spread for as long as Cole could remember.

Even when Cole's father was alive, Gunderson had put a sizeable offer on the table for the north pasture that butted up to his land. That was one of two times Cole had seen his father lose his temper. He'd nearly thrown the man and his son out of the McAllister kitchen. Of course, it was no secret to anyone who lived within a hundred miles that the

McAllisters and the Gundersons hadn't gotten along for over four generations. Cole wasn't sure if anyone recalled what had started the feud. Didn't matter. If and when the time came to sell, he'd sooner rob a bank than deed so much as a square inch to Wallace. Cole's dislike for the man had nothing to do with the family history. He simply couldn't abide the bastard's mistreatment of his animals.

The bunkhouse and barn came into view, made hazy by the plumes of gray smoke drifting up from the rows of barbecue pits. Chester had started early this morning, baking corn bread and preparing the chicken and ribs for this evening's bash. As Cole rode toward the stables, he saw the groups of picnic tables set up closer to the main house. A couple had been placed near the bunkhouse kitchen. White lights had been strung up around the pine trees and along the corral fence, and a rainbow of balloons bobbed from the posts.

He didn't see his brother's Jeep so Cole knew Jesse hadn't returned from the airport with Rachel yet. Some of the neighbors were already here. He recognized the two black-and-red trucks parked along the gravel driveway, and noticed that the Richardson brood and Ida and Henry Pickens were climbing out of their pickups on the other side of the barn. He didn't know how many people his mother had invited, over fifty he'd reckon. And that wasn't counting the hands—most of them had been as much a part of Rachel's life as Cole and his brothers.

If Cole hadn't stepped in, there would have been a much larger crowd. The shocked expression on his mother's face when he'd given her a budget remained vivid in his mind. What had stung even more was the sad, resigned nod that told him he suspected they were in trouble. Still, she hadn't asked for details, hadn't given him so much as a glance of disapproval or a hint of disappointment. Being the gracious lady she'd always been, she'd simply smiled and said how happy she would be to have Rachel home again, and that was all that mattered.

His sister would be a whole different story. She'd take one look at the barn that needed painting, the corral fence that should've been replaced by now and all the other areas he'd been forced to ignore, and she'd have questions, demand answers. He wouldn't blame her one bit. Didn't mean he'd welcome the inquisition.

SHORTLY AFTER TEN, the last of the guests started to leave. Cole normally would be getting into the sack by now since he routinely awoke at five every day, but throughout the evening he'd caught Rachel's questioning looks enough to know that she wouldn't wait until morning to give him the third degree.

Fighting the temptation to go help his brothers clear the tables, he stayed near the house, leaning on the clothesline post. He watched her tug a lock of Johnny Weaver's strawberry-blond hair. The boy stopped yawning long enough to give her a toothless grin.

"Time for someone to go to bed," she said, raising her brows when the youngster opened his mouth in protest.

Instead of arguing, Johnny yawned again.

His mother, Peggy, smiled at Rachel, then gave her a quick hug. "Good to have you back. You'll have to come for supper once you get settled."

"I'll do that." Rachel handed over the plate of leftover corn bread, chicken and chocolate cake she'd wrapped for Peggy to take, then swooped down and kissed the boy's cheek. He turned beet-red, but there was that grin again.

Cole nodded his goodbye to the Weavers and waited while Rachel walked them toward the driveway. She'd make a great mother some day. He knew that a family of her own was what she wanted eventually, but in the meantime, he had no doubt her focus would be on him and the Sundance.

He stared up at the clear summer sky filled with stars,

remembering how as a kid he'd lain on his back deep in the grass, hands clasped behind his head, gazing up at those very same stars making wishes that had rarely come true. Hadn't stopped him though. Especially after Lizzie Adams had finally laid a wet one on his mouth for a full three seconds. The unexpected memory made him smile.

The moment faded, and he wondered what had happened to that bright-eyed, optimistic young boy. Reality, bills, droughts, payroll…that's what had happened. And now Rachel, the little spitfire. The only girl and the youngest, but she was a force to be reckoned with, all right.

As soon as the Weavers' taillights burned red in the darkness, she walked purposefully toward him. Out of the corner of his eye he noticed that Jesse and Trace had stopped collecting the platters and bowls from the tables, as if waiting for the fireworks. Hell, had she already said something to them? Or had he been fooling himself about how much they knew of the family's trouble?

"Can I talk to you in your office for a minute?" Rachel asked, glancing over at their mother who paid them no attention as she helped Chester store the leftovers.

"Yep." Cole pushed off the post. "Looks like we might have company," he said, gesturing with his chin at his approaching brothers.

Jesse and Trace tried to make it look as if it was a coincidence that they were carrying the platters of food to the kitchen at that particular moment, but Cole knew otherwise. He didn't care. Better that they were included, and he could get this over with.

They all went inside and, after the brothers deposited their platters in the kitchen, they all headed for the office. Jesse claimed the brown leather couch, while Trace stretched his tall lanky body on the extra office chair that likely should've been tossed out years ago. Cole closed the door, not surprised that Rachel had chosen to stand. While he and his brothers all exceeded six feet, like every McAllister man before them, Rachel took after their mother, with her auburn hair, green eyes and petite frame. From early on she'd preferred to even her odds by standing over her brothers whenever they had a family meeting.

Cole obliged her by sinking into his chair behind the desk, then laid his head back on the black leather headrest. Might as well get comfortable. Rachel was like a dog with a bone once she set her mind on something, and she'd say her piece even if it took until midnight.

She met Cole's eyes. "What's going on?"

"You wanna be more specific?"

"This place…" She waved a hand, her gaze darting to the window. "It looks like hell."

"Nice, Rach." Trace snorted. "It's not as though we've been sitting around on our asses."

"That's not what I mean." She glared at Trace.

Cole and Jesse exchanged weary glances. Typically one of them would end up refereeing the pair of younger hotheads, but before the discussion heated up, Cole said, "Look, money's been tight. Cosmetics aren't a priority right now."

"I don't understand…" Rachel shook her head. "Did something happen?"

"Yeah, the economy dove nose-first down a sinkhole." Trace gave a helpless shrug. "We're not the only ones having trouble. I heard tonight that the Circle Four is filing for bankruptcy. Damn shame."

Cole scrubbed a hand over his face. He'd heard the news last week and decided to keep it to himself. No need to cause panic.

"Bankruptcy?" Rachel's eyes widened. When she moved to sit on the couch with Jesse, he reached over and rubbed her shoulder. "I don't think anyone around here has ever gone broke before. Do you think it's true?" she asked, her frightened gaze finding Cole.

"I wouldn't doubt it. The cost of shipping beef has put a drain on all of us. Expenses keep going up." Cole inhaled. "At least we haven't laid off anyone yet. Just about everyone else in the county has."

"Yet," Rachel murmured, her face growing pale. "How bad is it?" she asked. "For us, I mean."

Cole's insides twisted. No more hiding, no more white-washing the truth. Even if he wanted to, the bank ledger would call him a liar. "Bad. Real bad."

Trace abruptly turned his head, directed a probing look at Jesse, who remained impassive. He was a lot like Cole in that he kept his emotions in check, everything else close to the vest and spoke sparingly. After his discharge from the air force, Jesse had become even more circumspect.

Rachel's voice was shaky when she asked, "Does Mom know?"

"We haven't had any discussions, but she's not a stupid woman. I'm sure she's noticed the same things you have." Cole sighed. "Hell, the whole place needs improvements. So far, I've been able to keep the creditors off my back, but I can only trade on our reputation for so long."

"It's not fair to hide the problem from her."

At the hint of accusation in her tone, Jesse jumped in. "We're not hiding, just trying to survive. Why point out the obvious with no solution in sight?" He looked pointedly at Cole. "Creditors are on *our* backs, too, bro. This isn't only your problem. We all have a stake here."

Cole rubbed his jaw. Sure they all had a stake, that's why he felt so damn guilty. Because the responsibility to make the place profitable was his alone.

Trace fidgeted, loosening the collar of his blue Western-cut shirt. What the hell was he looking guilty about? This wasn't his fault. Not just because he was still young. Maybe he was feeling sheepish for not understanding the depth of their problem. But the failure of the ranch was on Cole, always had been. He didn't deny it.

He shifted to find Jesse staring grimly at him. "Jesus, you think you're to blame?" Jesse shook his head in disbelief. "You arrogant bastard."

"Screw you. You know Dad left—"

"Stop it." Rachel stared at them in equal measure. "What's wrong with you two?"

Cole just smiled. This was his and Jesse's way of keeping each other in check. They didn't mean anything. Rachel must've forgotten. She didn't relax her clenched fists until Jesse grunted out a laugh.

Rachel rolled her eyes. "Okay, you two Neanderthals, here's the thing. I understand the economy sucks, but I don't buy that there's no solution." She paused, and no one seemed eager to end the silence. Hunching her shoulders, she seemed to crawl into herself. "Oh, God, I spent all that money on graduate school... You should've told me."

"Come on," Cole said. "Knock that off."

Jesse elbowed her. "I used money for school, too."

"Those were the old days when we could afford it."

"Old days, huh?" Jesse looped an arm around her neck and mussed her hair. "You little squirt."

"You know what I mean." She shoved him until he released her from the headlock.

Cole wouldn't argue the age issue. At thirty-two he felt older than dirt. Jesse was only a year younger, but Cole suspected his brother had already seen more than most men saw in a lifetime.

Rachel set her sights on Trace. "Was the lack of money the reason you chose not to go to college?" she asked, her voice soft and miserable.

"No." He made a face. "I hate classrooms and staying indoors all day. You know that." He plowed a hand through his longish dark hair. "I'm sorry, Cole, I knew we were postponing repairs and holding on to equipment, but I guess I didn't want to see how bad it was. Bet you wanted to kick me to next Sunday when I asked for a new truck a few months back."

Cole shook his head. "You're twenty-six. 'Course you want a new truck."

"Okay…" Rachel straightened. "So let's talk about what we need to do to get back on our feet."

Cole smiled patiently at the family optimist. "It's not that simple. Too many factors are out of our control."

"Such as?"

"High diesel-fuel costs, consumers' shrinking grocery budgets. Corn has gone way up because so much of the crop is going for ethanol…" He continued while she listened intently, nodding occasionally and not once interrupting.

His speech went on longer than he'd intended, maybe because it felt good to release some of the pressure, but he cut himself off when he saw the depressed expression on Trace's face. Jesse had slumped deeper into the couch and stared at his boots. Only Rachel looked unbowed. She sat forward, her green eyes sparkling and ready to do battle.

"I have an idea—" she said thoughtfully "—that just might solve our problems…at least in the short term…and who knows, maybe for the long term, as well."

Cole tamped down his amusement. Although he was all for her participation, she was about to learn there was no easy answer. "What's that?"

"Don't say anything until I'm finished because it won't cost much to get started—"

"Rachel, wait, stop. We don't have any money. I don't know how to say it more plainly."

She put up her hands. "Hear me out."

"All right," Cole said, his jaw clenched. Jesus, he'd thought it was a kindness to spare the women useless worry. Obviously he was wrong. Rachel couldn't seem to process the ugly truth.

"I've had this thought for a while, a couple of years really—ever since my sorority sisters went all gaga over the pictures of the Sundance on my screen saver slide show." A big smile stretched across her flushed face. "What would you think about starting a dude ranch?"

Thunderstruck, Cole and Jesse stared at her.

Trace snorted. "A what?"

"A dude ranch. You know…kind of like a big bed-and-breakfast where people come for vacation and go on trail rides and watch rodeos, have cookouts, go white-water rafting and—"

"I understand what a dude ranch is," Trace said with disgust. "I'm trying to figure out if you've gone loco."

Rachel pressed her lips together, and then calmly said, "I'm not surprised at your reaction." She looked from Trace to Cole to Jesse. "But we have plenty of extra room we don't even use, a whole separate wing of the house, in fact, and there won't be much start-up cost because we already have everything right here."

"This is a cattle ranch," Cole said quietly, even though he was with Trace; their sister was nuts. "We don't know the first thing about catering to folks used to living with conveniences, and we can't afford the extra help."

"Mom, Hilda and I can take care of the rooms and meals. Trace and the hands can take turns providing the outings," she said, and Trace groaned, then muttered an oath. Without missing a beat, Rachel continued, "I'll do all the advertising and bookings online, which will cost next to nothing, and I'll design the website. I'm very good at it. We might even be able to attract sponsors to help cover costs."

Cole shook his head. "The place needs painting, we'll need insurance and trying to sidestep kids running around will only—"

Trace grunted. "I like kids well enough, but city folk don't seem to get it—they'll be underfoot while we're trying to work...."

"How about we don't accept kids?" Rachel said. "Maybe later we'll expand to families, but for now I'm thinking we should cater to single women. They'd be much simpler to accommodate. Plus I know how to push all the right buttons to have them lining up to make a reservation."

"Shit, you're out of your mind," Jesse murmured, and Cole couldn't even speak he was so flabbergasted.

"Hey, wait a minute." Trace's eyes sharpened with new interest. "Let Rachel finish."

Her lips lifted in a triumphant smile. "I figured that way the hands wouldn't balk too much, either."

"No," Cole said flatly.

His sister's flash of disappointment transformed into a glare of pure challenge. "You have a better idea?"

Cole cleared his throat. He sure hadn't expected this confrontation so soon. "I have one, but I figured we could do some brainstorming."

Rachel folded her arms across her chest. "Yet you're quick to shoot me down."

"Your suggestion isn't practical," Cole said irritably. "And you know that."

Trace shrugged. "I kind of like Rachel's way of thinking."

Cole and Jesse both gave him a long, blistering look.

"Well, big brother, what's your idea?" Rachel caught and held Cole's gaze. "We're all listening."

Cole breathed in deeply. "There's a couple of hundred acres running south of the creek that we haven't used for years. Tell you the truth, I can't see it ever being much use to us and..."

Three pairs of wounded eyes stared at him as if he'd just committed high treason. Jesse spoke first, his voice thick with denial. "You're not saying we should sell McAllister land."

The door creaked open. They all turned their heads and

watched their mother slowly cross the threshold. Her devastated expression erased any doubt that she'd been listening.

"No," Cole said, the bitter taste of defeat coating the inside of his mouth. "Guess I'm not." His gaze moved back to Rachel, who had the good grace not to smirk.

2

JAMIE DANIELS PICKED UP the lavender taffeta dress she'd never wear again even if she lived to be a hundred, and carried it to her closet. What had Linda been thinking when she'd chosen the frilly ruffled concoction? And for an August afternoon wedding in Los Angeles? Jamie's jaw had about hit the floor the day her friend had marshaled her and the other two bridesmaids to the bridal shop to get their opinion.

It wasn't as if Jamie had held back, she'd been as tactful as she knew how to be considering all three selections had been pretty horrific. Linda had wanted purple and ruffles and there'd been no getting around it. Jill and Kaylee had both tied the knot several months before and had been more zen about the whole thing. Apparently they had the same "perfect wedding" gene, where nothing, not even good taste, was allowed to alter one single piece of the dream.

Sighing, Jamie hung the lavender dress behind the other bridesmaids' dresses at the far end of her walk-in closet. The blue one she could probably wear again to a fancy cocktail reception, but the other two she'd keep for a respectable length of time and then donate them to a worthy charity to help make some other woman's silly dream come true.

Good God, when had she become so jaded? Just because

she hadn't given marriage a thought, it didn't mean the wedding tradition was silly. Besides, she was happy for her two friends and her cousin Kaylee. She was. Really. She just wished she didn't suddenly feel so damn alone.

She drew in a deep breath, a bit surprised that she'd allowed herself the admission. Of course it didn't matter, because she'd rebound soon. She always did. She'd learned survival at an early age. Her parents were diplomats. They traveled extensively, which meant she'd traveled, changed schools, changed friends, adopted new languages, adapted to different customs. Her unconventional childhood had turned her into a chameleon.

Ironically, it was during the three years she'd been sent back to the States to live with her aunt Liz, uncle Philip and cousin Kaylee on their Georgia farm that Jamie had had the most trouble adjusting. Mainly because for the first nine years of her life she'd never been separated from her parents for more than a few days. But then the embassy where they'd worked had come under attack and before she knew it she'd been strapped into a seat on a military plane, by herself. And no amount of tears and begging had stopped her parents from sending her away.

She still remembered staring out the window as the plane ascended, watching the gray smoke rise from the city below, convinced she'd never see her mother and father again. Oh, she had seen them all right, a year later…for a mere week before they'd returned to the lion's den. Though the fighting was over, the tensions had remained high in that part of the world and it was decided she'd stay in Georgia until they were assigned another post.

They'd done their job as parents and protected her from harm. Both of them were crazy smart with Ivy League educations, the works. But they'd failed to see that a child could suffer more than physical damage. They'd chosen their careers over her, and she'd spent three years wondering if they'd found that they preferred being childless. On her twelfth birthday they'd surprised her by showing up at the farm and whisking her away to their new post in Singapore. Two years later she was shipped off to boarding school and her relationship with them had never been the same.

Why in the world was she thinking about all this now? Maybe too much champagne at the wedding reception. She never did care for bubbly, not even the really good stuff, but she'd drunk her share of mimosas because, wow, had it been warm all afternoon.

Pulling her hair off her neck, she moved to the window and stared out at the Los Angeles skyline. She loved her condo smack-dab in the middle of West L.A., even though she wasn't home much. When she wasn't gallivanting about the globe, gathering interesting tidbits for her travel blog, she adored holing up for days at a time with a few pints of Häagen-Dazs, leaving only to go for a dip in the rooftop pool or for a workout in the building's fitness club.

The trouble was, for six years, Linda, Jill and Kaylee had all lived within a five-mile radius of her. One or all three of them would pop over for lunch or lure her out for a last-minute drink at the Beverly Hilton. Now they were all married, relocated to the Valley. Well, Linda hadn't moved yet, but it was only a matter of time.

Jolted by the sudden ache of loneliness that swept through her, Jamie pressed her forehead to the glass. Her vision blurred a little and she blinked to clear it. Now who was she going to call at one in the morning to complain about a bad date? Or to squeal over a totally hot guy that she'd met at the airport? Who would she take on trips? Sometimes Jill had gone with her to Europe or Canada, while Kaylee had preferred the Asian getaways.

Straightening, Jamie smiled, remembering the Mississippi River houseboat she'd rented for two weeks. She couldn't recall how she'd talked Linda into that fiasco but, man, had they laughed…so hard sometimes that it hurt. Amazing they'd both survived their ineptness on the water. But in the end they'd agreed they'd had a fabulous time seeing parts of the South they never would've seen otherwise, meeting incredible people, eating ridiculously yummy deep-fried food she'd never dreamed would touch her lips.

That particular adventure had elevated her blog to the million-hits level. After that her numbers kept climbing and she'd attracted enough paying advertisers to carve out a nice niche for herself. Only twenty-eight and living the dream. She couldn't ask for more.…

Dammit, she wanted her friends back.

Yeah, she knew she was being a whiny baby, but tough. The girls were more than friends, they'd become her family. Her parents still lived in Europe, and Aunt Liz and Uncle Philip had been great to her, always welcoming her for holidays, or anytime. But her buddies had been her sounding board, the place she'd turned for advice or when she'd needed a shoulder to sob on since freshman year of college. Kaylee was a year younger but she and Jamie had grown so close that she'd followed Jamie to UCLA.

Jamie rubbed her eyes, wishing she were more tired. Sleep would erase some of the edginess. Turning from the window, her gaze went to the handmade mahogany clock she'd picked up in Indonesia last year. Bad enough it was only midnight… she'd been back from Hawaii for three days and hadn't completely adjusted to the time difference.

Work. That was the escape she needed. Anyway, her blog post was due tomorrow. Unfortunately her next trip wasn't scheduled for another three weeks. Stupid move on her part. She should've foreseen tonight.

Jill had married first, and as soon as the reception was over, Kaylee, Linda and Jamie had headed for the closest bar and gotten tipsy while they retold college dating stories and mourned the passing of their old life. A few months later a former boyfriend of Kaylee's had shown up. Within weeks he'd shocked everyone by popping the question. Kaylee's answer had been twice as shocking. Dan had never been on Jamie's short list of favorite people, or long list for that matter, but she sucked up her disappointment and put on a happy face for her cousin's sake.

Then it was just Jamie and Linda drinking at the Crown and haggling over where to eat or what movie to see when Jamie was in town.

And now...

She exhaled sharply and quickly flipped open her laptop. She distracted herself by checking comments on her blog, catching up on Twitter and replying to her mother's perfunctory bi-monthly email. About to tackle tomorrow's blog post, she noticed the banner ad for the Sundance Dude Ranch in Blackfoot Falls, Montana.

A dude ranch. One of her regular readers had mentioned something about a dude ranch just last week. It wasn't this ranch, but there was something about the ad that caught Jamie's attention.

"Huh."

She clicked on the website link and immediately clear blue sky, gorgeous mountains and tall Douglas firs flooded the screen. In the foreground was a large three-story log-style house with a wraparound porch complete with a swing and rocking chairs. So peaceful and homey-looking. Kind of reminded her of her aunt and uncle's peanut farm.

Why hadn't she tried a dude ranch before? It was different from anything she'd done, and she'd never been to Montana, although she'd heard it was beautiful country. Her readers would love it.

Leaning way back in her comfy office chair, she smiled and got busy clicking. She learned that it was a working ranch owned by the McAllister family since the late 1800s, then she checked out pictures of the adjacent national forest and wilderness area and skimmed the list of activities. She already knew how to ride pretty well and she'd gone white-water rafting twice. But there were other things that caught her interest, like rodeos, guided hikes, overnight pack trips, cattle driving and…

And them.

She bolted upright, causing her chair to roll backward on the bamboo floor mat. Grabbing the edge of her desk, she pulled herself in, then peered closer at the rugged-looking, dark-haired cowboys sitting on great big horses. Squinting, she hoped for a better look at their faces. Which was absurd, but it didn't stop her from trying.

Holy crap, Cole McAllister was friggin' hot. With his wide shoulders, long lean legs and brooding expression, the man was a wet dream. Jesse McAllister, with his Stetson pulled low, had the smoldering thing down pat. Oh, and she had brother Trace pegged in a flash, despite the lack of detail in the photograph. He was a hottie who knew it, and wasn't in the market for taming.

Brilliant ad, really. The bad-boys-of-the-West image against the blue sky and snowcapped mountains, so innately gorgeous in those worn jeans and Western shirts they fulfilled every single cowboy fantasy in the book. Jamie would be shocked if the dude ranch wasn't sold out for the first six months.

But, she was still going to try to get in. The sooner the better. Even though the ranch had been around forever, opening up for guests was a new business for the family. Tomorrow started their second week of operation.

She clicked on the calendar, saw there were two available bookings left, and got out her credit card. Oh, boy, her readers were going to love those cowboys. Hell, she was halfway there herself.

CALM AS COULD BE, Rachel was setting a pitcher of lemonade and a plate of cookies on the porch table as Cole rode up to the house. What in the Sam Hill was she up to? He'd received an urgent text from her while riding the east fence and had ridden hard for nearly twenty minutes to get here.

"Is Mom okay?" he asked, swinging off Tango and jumping to the ground.

"What?" Rachel frowned briefly. "Oh, she's fine."

A female guest chose that moment to walk out the front door, and Cole groaned to himself. He'd done everything he could, short of working twenty-four-hour days, to stay away from the place since the first group of guests had arrived twelve days ago. Eight altogether, all of them women. Jesus. The hands were barely getting their chores done.

"Afternoon, ma'am," he said politely, touching the brim of his hat. She gave him a flirty smile, and he turned back to his sister, not bothering to hide his irritation.

She missed it, too busy showing all her teeth to the guest. "Hi, Kim." Rachel gestured toward the barn. "Dutchy and the rest of the girls are waiting for you to join them on a trail ride."

The woman lingered a moment, and Cole could feel her gaze on him, but he'd enter the house with his dusty boots on before he gave her an opening. She finally pushed on, the impractical heels of her city boots clicking down the wooden steps.

He knew the instant he was safe from the blonde but not from his sister.

Rachel lost her smile and glared at him. "You have to start being nicer to these women," she said in an angry murmur.

"I don't have to do anything." He'd given in enough, even helped freshen up the porch with a coat of redwood stain, scraped up enough money to spruce up the barn and kept his mouth shut when Rachel had ordered a wagonload of flowers for the rock beds. "If I wasn't pleasant enough for you, then don't drag me back in the middle of the damn afternoon. What did you want, anyway?"

"Do you know how much money we've taken in for deposits?"

Yeah, it had barely covered the cost to ready the place. Grunting, he helped himself to a glass and the pitcher of lemonade.

"No, that's for our guests." She snatched both out of his hands. "We have six arrivals in the next hour."

Cole looked up at the ceiling in disgust, noticed a spot he'd missed in his all-fired hurry for the opening day. "Lord, give me patience."

"You'd do well to pray a little harder." Rachel offered him a cookie on a small, fancy pink napkin and gave him one of those sneaky smiles that said she wanted something.

He put up his hands, backed away from her. "No."

"You love oatmeal raisin."

"No to whatever it is you're gonna ask me."

She grabbed his forearm and slapped the cookie onto his palm. "Jamie Daniels is arriving any minute. She's a very popular travel blogger and we're damn lucky to have her. If she likes this place, business will boom. I want you here with me to greet her."

Cole barked out a laugh, shook his head and glanced toward the driveway. No dust coming from the road. He was still safe. Maybe even had enough time to run in for a drink of water and grab a sandwich before he lit out for the north pasture.

"Don't you dare."

"What?"

"I know that look. You're planning your escape." Rachel's lower lip jutted out in that annoying sulk. She was his baby sister and sometimes it was hard saying no to her. "I've put a lot of time and effort into making this dude ranch work. Can I get a little help here?"

He stared at her, not sure if he was disappointed, surprised or just plain angry. Sighing, he removed his hat and used the back of his sleeve to wipe his forehead.

"Oh, Cole." Rachel briefly covered her mouth. "What a horrible thing for me to say. You've given your whole life to this place. No one has worked harder than you, not even Jesse, and certainly not me or Trace."

"Enough." He squinted toward the midafternoon sun. "I'm going inside to wash up a bit, get something to eat. Maybe I'll still be around when your guest arrives."

JAMIE HAD OBVIOUSLY made a wrong turn. Odd, because she was good with maps, but she should've gotten to the Sundance by now. With a surge of gratitude, she steered the rental car into the gas station that seemed to have appeared out of nowhere. Wow, did she have to pee. After that she'd get directions. She had to be close to the ranch but after miles and miles of nothing but blue sky and distant mountains, she wasn't willing to trust herself, the map or the car's useless navigation system.

As much as she despised gas-station restrooms—and this one looked like something out of the 1930s—she was in no position to be picky, so she coasted around to the side until she spotted a sign. She hurriedly got out of the car, grabbing her purse and keys.

The bathroom door was locked.

"Dammit." What the hell… Were they afraid someone would break in and clean it?

She tried not even to breathe as she went around to the front. No sign of life. Two parked trucks, though. Someone had to be around. She couldn't see through the window or past the ads for jerky and different soft drinks plastered to the glass. The doorknob looked grimy, but she was saved from having to touch it when the door abruptly flew open.

"Looking for this?" A young man, late teens, grinning, held up a hoop with a key dangling from it.

"Thank you," she said, unceremoniously grabbing it and hurrying back to the restroom.

One stall, unisex, could be cleaner, but she didn't care at this point. With the tissues she kept in her purse, she covered the seat, did her business, then, while she washed her hands, stared glumly into the cloudy wall mirror barely larger than an index card. She was a mess. Too little sleep the past few nights and then today…getting here had been a nightmare. Two flights, an hour-and-a-half layover, then another hour-plus of driving.

She shook out her wet hands, deciding to use the car mirror to touch up her eye makeup and lip gloss. As soon as she stepped outside, she saw a thin older man wearing dirty coveralls circling the rental car, and appearing far too interested in the luggage she'd thrown on the backseat.

"May I help you?" she asked, hitching her purse strap up securely on her shoulder.

He raised his piercing gaze to her face, his dark brows pulled together in a suspicious frown. "Where you headed?"

She hesitated, tempted to say something about his bad manners. But the lanky young man who'd given her the key rounded the corner of the building just in time.

"Thank you," she said, returning the key. "Are the pumps self-serve?"

"Pull your car up and I'll take care of it for you, ma'am." He smiled, then studiously eyed the other man. "Got your tires ordered, Avery. They should be in next Friday."

The older man ignored him, his interest still firmly planted on her. "Didn't catch where you're headed."

Jamie sighed and opened the car door. She was going to ask for directions anyway. Besides, the kid knew him. "The Sundance. Do you know where it is?"

He moved his head to the side and spat on the pavement.

She just smiled. If he'd intended to gross her out she had news for him. There were still restaurants on the other side of the world where men used spittoons. "Was that a no?"

"Don't mind him. I'm Billy," the teenager said, grinning. "You're looking for the McAllisters' new dude ranch."

"I am."

"Stay on the road for another five miles. You'll see a sign for Blackfoot Falls. Take the next left after that. The road's not so good but you'll do fine."

Billy had already started backing toward the pumps so she closed her door, then pulled the compact around the building. She ignored Avery except for a brief glance in the rearview mirror. He followed close behind, but she wasn't so much afraid as annoyed. The old-timer probably didn't like tourists. Nothing new there, either. There was always someone fighting the idea of strangers poking around.

She parked and lowered her window. Billy confirmed that she wanted the medium-grade gas, then started topping off her tank, which didn't require much, but she had used their restroom after all.

"Hey, Billy? Got a question for you."

He looked up. "Ma'am?"

"My name is Jamie, by the way. Are there any other dude ranches in the area?"

"Nope. This is the first. Only been open a week so we haven't seen many visitors yet. Heard they're taking on people clear through the fall, though."

From behind her, Avery muttered a curse.

Jamie jumped because she hadn't realized he'd been standing near the compact's bumper.

"Don't mind him. He just don't like strangers." Billy shot the man a look of disgust. "Pretty sorry thing when I gotta remind my elder to mind his manners."

"No good is gonna come of that dude ranch business, I tell ya," Avery grumbled. "This is cattle country. Always was, always will be. We've had hard times before and we rode it out. You youngsters are too damn impatient." He spat again and then ambled toward a dusty dark green pickup.

Shaking his head, Billy pulled the nozzle out of the tank and returned it to the pump. "He's not the only one upset with the McAllisters." He took a rag from his back pocket and wiped his hands. "That'll be nine dollars even."

"Why?" Jamie passed him a ten, motioned for him to keep the change.

He blinked, not looking eager to volunteer more information. Finally shrugging, he said, "Some folks feel like Avery. They don't want outsiders poking around. The other half hopes it'll bring business to the town and no more stores will have to shut down."

She gave him a reassuring smile. "Everyone is having problems. I travel for a living and it's not pretty out there."

"Yeah, I know, but the McAllisters...they're like...let's just say everyone was kinda shocked when Cole had to turn away help." Billy chuckled. "Though not as shocked as when they found out Rachel had talked him into the dude ranch."

"Rachel...the sister, right?"

Billy's smile faded, and he flushed. "I shouldn't be talkin' about the McAllisters," he mumbled. "They're good people. The best." He backed away. "You have a nice time over there."

"I will." She smiled, then pulled back onto the highway.

She found the sign to Blackfoot Falls with no problem and turned onto the road, which after a couple of miles went from rutting pavement to rough gravel. Obviously the dude ranch idea was a recent one or they might have done something about this road. She didn't care, though, especially when she saw the overhead iron sign strung between two poles, announcing the Sundance.

Jamie turned onto yet another gravel road, and the spectacular view of the Rockies in the background nearly stole her breath. Knowing she was on the right track, she looked her fill. Within minutes she saw a group of buildings, several trucks... As she got closer, she noticed three women, one of them wearing a pink sundress, laughing with a couple of cowboys.

She squinted to see if she recognized any of the brothers, but it was dusty and her gaze got caught on the sprawling house itself. It was beautiful, huge and looked exactly like the pictures in the online brochure. But it was the tall, lean cowboy standing near the porch that had her heart doing a cartwheel.

3

"I THINK IT'S HER because everyone else booked in pairs," Rachel said, trying to look casual as the small red Ford nosed its way toward the house. She elbowed Cole in the ribs. "So don't be rude."

Cole glanced at his sister. "When have you ever known me to be rude?"

"At the harvest dance five years ago when Maggie Johnson pinched your ass."

"That was self-defense."

Rachel chuckled. "She thought she was going to marry you."

"Where the hell did she get that idea?" He tugged down the rim of his hat so he could look without the lady knowing he was eyeing her. No sense her getting any wrong ideas right out of the chute. Only natural he was curious. Quite an assortment of young ladies had been parading around the ranch for the past week. Some real pretty, but most of them kind of silly.

"Mmm, might have been me."

He turned from watching the Daniels woman park her car and stared at his sister. "You better be joking."

"We were fourteen when I told her that. She should've gotten over it by then and married Paul Haas," Rachel muttered, and walked toward the car.

Cole stayed where he was, able to get only a vague glimpse of the new guest through her car's tinted-glass windows. The driver's door opened, and she climbed out, the sun catching the gold in her tawny hair, which was pulled back into a ponytail.

The open door blocked a good part of his view as she shook hands with Rachel. She matched his sister's height of about five-five, and he could see the woman had a pleasing profile and the good sense to wear jeans. Boots, too, worn ones— not the impractical high-heeled pointy kind so many of the guests had shown up wearing.

Rachel indicated the parking area on the east side of the barn, and the woman lifted her hand to shade her eyes. No flash of some god-awful color on her fingernails. Already she'd risen in his esteem, but that didn't mean he'd offer more than this meet-and-greet. He'd made it clear from the get-go. The dude ranch was Rachel's baby. He had better things to do.

Stepping away from the car, Rachel waved him over. His reluctance ebbed when she motioned to the trunk and he realized she wanted his help carrying in luggage. Adjusting his hat, he strolled over, wishing he'd changed his dusty blue work shirt. He almost stumbled at the errant thought. Hell, he'd insisted Rachel advertise the place as a working ranch and since he seemed to be the only person at the Sundance paying more attention to the cattle than the females, he wasn't about to put on airs.

"Jamie, this is my brother, Cole. He's the oldest, a bit ornery and stubborn, but a real nice guy when you get to know him."

Cole tightened his jaw, did his fair best not to react. But he and sis needed to have another little talk. Though Rachel's light laugh said she already knew she'd irritated him.

Their new guest laughed, too. "I don't have any brothers

but I'm guessing you just earned yourself an earful." She offered him her hand just as she had done with Rachel. "I'm
Jamie Daniels, and I'm looking forward to getting to know
you, Cole McAllister."

That wouldn't happen. "Pleased to meet you, ma'am." He
touched the brim of his hat, then pressed his palm to hers,
which was soft and small while his was rough and callused.

She held on a few seconds longer than he expected. "Did
you know that in ancient times men shook hands to show
they weren't hiding a weapon?" Her hazel eyes sparkled with
mischief. She let go, lifted her hands, palms out, and glanced
down at herself. "Not carrying, promise, no need to call me
ma'am."

Cole blinked; that was the best he could do to keep from
staring at the tempting swell of her breasts, the small waist,
flat belly, the way her hips curved out enough to fill a man's
hands when he took her…

"Sure…" He silently cleared his dry throat, moved a cautious step away. "Jamie, uh, you wanna pop the trunk?"

"Everything I brought is right here." She opened the back
door, then leaned in to grab a duffel-style leather bag.

His gaze went straight to her shapely backside. It wasn't
as if he'd had a choice. The way she was bending over, her
hind end angled up…and he was a man, after all. The sudden
feeling that he was being watched made him glance over to
see Rachel standing by the hood, regarding him with wide-
eyed curiosity.

He sent her a warning look, then shifted his attention back
to getting her guest inside so he could be on his way. "Let
me get that," he said, and received a shock all the way to his
toes when unthinkingly he nearly grabbed Jamie by the hips
to move her aside.

Christ almighty.

He jumped back, waited for her to get clear. "Maybe you
wouldn't mind moving the car while I take your bag inside,"

he murmured, and out of the corner of his eye caught her smile.

"Will do. Thanks."

"You know which room?" Rachel asked as he lifted the bag from the backseat.

He didn't like the devilish tone of her voice. "No, you'd better come show me."

"After I move the car," Jamie said, "I'll meet you inside, if that's all right?"

"Perfect." Rachel hitched a thumb over her shoulder. "There's cold lemonade and cookies on the porch. Help yourself, then come on in."

Cole hefted the bag and closed the car door. Rachel trailed him inside, and when he headed for the kitchen stairs that their housekeeper, Hilda, and the guests used, Rachel stopped him.

"I gave Jamie the room next to yours," she said, then breezily passed him as if the change of plans didn't matter.

"You hold on there." He stood stubbornly in the big foyer, and waited for her to face him.

She'd already made it partway up the main staircase but she turned, her expression all innocence.

"You're already reneging on our deal?"

"What deal?"

"Dammit, Rachel." He set down the bag, exhaled sharply. "We agreed no guests in the main part of the house."

"Yes, we did. But number one, we're full, and number two, this is Jamie Daniels we're talking about." Rachel's gaze drifted to the window, and then, in a muted voice, she added, "We can't talk about this now."

"And you had the nerve to call me ornery? You sneaky little cuss. If you think you're gonna bushwhack me like this—"

"What's going on?" Hilda pushed through the swinging doors between the dining room and kitchen.

Barbara McAllister was right behind her. "You two hush up. We have guests."

"A fact about which I'm painfully aware." Cole dialed down his tone but continued to glare at Rachel. "This little pipsqueak has taken it in her mind to give up the family's privacy."

After a short silence, his mother sniffed and quietly said, "It is Jamie Daniels, after all."

Hilda added her agreement.

Cole shifted his disbelieving gaze to the two older conspirators, who gave him small guilty smiles.

Rachel said, "You didn't seem to mind her too much when she was bending across her backseat."

He turned back to glare at his sister, but damned if he could think of anything to say. So he pulled his gloves out of his rear pocket and started pulling one on. "You can take this bag up yourself."

"Wait," Rachel called after him as he headed for the swinging doors. "Mom, tell him not to leave yet."

He brushed past Hilda and his mother, ignoring their soft pleas, determined to escape through the kitchen door. "Women," he muttered, and refused to look back.

JAMIE DIDN'T WASTE much time unpacking. With all the traveling she did, she was an expert at hauling only what she needed. Besides, she was pretty anxious to see that cowboy again.

Cole was even better-looking in person with those bedroom brown eyes and sexy mouth. His dark hair was a bit too long, but she suspected it was more due to indifference than anything else. She sure looked forward to seeing him without the hat, although when he'd casually touched the brim in greeting, her silly heart had done a little curtsy.

Her guess was he'd shaved early this morning, but already stubble had shadowed his strong jaw. At first she'd thought he had a cleft in his chin but then she'd realized it was a small scar—which totally worked for her. The man was the real thing, all right. The kind of cowboy who might star in a fantasy or two. She wondered if a roll in the hay was as uncomfortable as it sounded.

Rachel had invited her to go on a tour as soon as Jamie had settled in, all the more reason she'd hurried stuffing her underwear, sleep shirts and jeans into the antique oak dresser, then hung up her blouses and sundress to loosen any wrinkles.

She glanced back at the neat homey room with the queen bed, hand-carved oak headboard, and blue-and-white patchwork quilt. Nice. She wondered how long the furniture had been in the family. Pulling the door closed, she counted five more rooms besides the two she knew were bathrooms. It was kind of weird to be staying on the same floor with the family. Rachel had explained that the rooms over the kitchen had been added to the house during the last renovation and were the designated guest areas but they were full and she hoped Jamie didn't mind.

Jamie didn't, not really. In fact it had to be harder for the McAllisters to have a stranger in their midst. Didn't stop her from wondering which room belonged to Cole. She was even more curious about his role in the dude ranch. She'd gotten a feeling from Billy at the gas station that this was Rachel's brainchild and her enthusiasm might not extend to the rest of the family.

At the top of the stairs, Jamie paused, unprepared for the breathtaking view of the Rocky Mountains. How had she not noticed the two-story vertical window? It didn't particularly suit the log-cabin style and yet it did because not to showcase the view would've been criminal.

"You're quick."

Jamie recognized Rachel's voice and looked down to see her approaching from the dining-room area.

"Yeah, I travel so much I kind of have to be." She took another step down, her attention divided between Rachel and the view. Against the distant clear blue sky an eagle soared.

"Amazing, isn't it?" Rachel had turned to the window.

"Do you ever take it for granted?"

"Nope. While I was away at school I'd come back for the summer and holidays and every time I'd be in total awe." She smiled. "My sorority sisters' reaction to the pictures on my laptop gave me the idea for the dude ranch. In fact, two of them are coming next month."

"Was it the pictures of the countryside or your brothers that got their attention?"

Rachel let out a surprised laugh, and Jamie truly wished she hadn't been quite so frank. Especially when an older woman came through the swinging doors with a knowing smile on her face. She had to be Rachel's mother. Same auburn hair, friendly green eyes, slight build.

Maybe she hadn't overheard.

"So which one of my brothers hooked you in?" Rachel asked, still grinning.

Jamie sighed. "I was just saying…" She left the last step and smiled sheepishly at the older woman. "Hi. You have to be Rachel's mom."

"It's Barbara." She set the vase of giant sunflowers on the foyer table and wiped her palms on the front of her jeans. "Yes, I'm the mother of the whole brood." She had a firm handshake and warm smile. "Dinner isn't for a couple of hours. May we get you a snack to hold you over?"

"Thanks, but I already had a couple of the oatmeal cookies. My compliments to whoever made them. Wow."

"I'll be sure to tell Cole," Rachel said.

Jamie blinked. "Seriously?"

Barbara made a tsking sound and gave her daughter an admonishing look.

Jamie chuckled, mostly at herself. What the hell, she'd already stuck her foot in it. "You got me all excited. I was ready to ask for his hand."

"You have my blessing," Barbara said, then laughed. "But I wouldn't count on it." She darted a look at Rachel. "I can't seem to get rid of any of them."

Rachel rolled her eyes. "Love you, Mom, but you're full of beans. What would you do without us?" She gave Barbara a quick kiss on the cheek. "Ready for the tour, Jamie?"

"Ready," she confirmed, the affection between mother and daughter tugging at her heart. She couldn't imagine her mom teasing her that way. They didn't have that kind of relationship. Sadly, they barely had one at all. "Rachel, if you're busy, I don't mind wandering around on my own."

"Nope, you're getting a tour. Otherwise, I'd have to help with dinner preparation."

"See you two later." With an indulgent smile, Barbara left through the swinging doors.

Rachel pointed out the kitchen and the large room with an impressive stone fireplace where guests tended to linger after dinner. At six, beer and margaritas would be served on the porch, dinner at seven in the dining room—with the exception of Saturday nights when Chester, the bunkhouse cook, fired up the smokers and the evening meal was served family-style on the picnic tables outside.

On their way to the stables, Jamie kept an eye out for Cole. A dark-haired man riding a bay horse left the barn and galloped north but it wasn't him. Even from the back Jamie would've known.

"The bunkhouse?" she asked, casting a glance at the two men leaving a long rectangular building across the yard. With the door open, a strong whiff of coffee drifted through the warm air and stirred an old memory. The men who worked her uncle's peanut farm always had a pot of acrid brew going, no matter how hot or humid the weather.

"It is, but I promised the hands we'd keep the place off-limits to guests. Believe me, you don't want to go in there anyway."

The men saw them and each lifted a hand in a half-hearted wave. Jamie smiled and nodded. "Must be hard for these guys to have a bunch of tourists underfoot."

"No, not at all," Rachel said quickly, then eyed the taller, more taciturn-looking man in his mid-sixties as the pair of cowhands moved closer. "Some of the old-timers are a little slow to adjust, but I promise it won't affect your stay here."

"I get it." Jamie shrugged. "It's a working ranch, and frankly, that's part of the appeal."

"I hope you're right," Rachel murmured, then as if regretting the remark, glanced at Jamie. "Everything is still new for us. I kind of wish you'd wanted to come later."

"Hey, don't worry about it." She smiled at Rachel, whom she'd decided she really liked. Had they met in college, Jamie suspected they would've been friends. "Look," she said, nudging her chin toward two giggly young women dressed inappropriately in heeled sandals, brief shorts and halter tops, watching a tall cowboy demonstrate a lassoing technique. "They seem to be having a good time."

"Oh, yeah. So is he, apparently. That's my brother Trace."

At Rachel's dry tone, Jamie grinned and got a better look at the guy's face. She could see now that he was one of the brothers. He was kind of young and good-looking but not in the same league as Cole...who she really wanted to see again. But she didn't dare ask, not after making that glib remark in front of his mother and sister.

"How do I sign up for activities?" she asked as they reached the stables.

"What specifically are you interested in?"

"As many things as I can fit into this week."

"Good for you. How about we go over the schedule after dinner?"

"Sure, and by the way, I'm not afraid of getting my hands dirty."

Rachel gave her a long speculative look, then absently nodded, a slow smile lifting her mouth. "I'll keep that in mind."

The stable was cool and dim after walking a few minutes in the blazing August sun. Horses stopped munching hay to curiously study the newcomer. Only a small paint seemed put off at the intrusion and tossed its mane, nickering loudly.

"Be quiet, Bubblegum." Rachel stopped at the stall and stroked the horse's neck. "Mind your manners."

Unexpectedly overcome by the familiar smells of fresh straw, leather and saddle soap, Jamie hesitated, reliving that moment nearly twenty years ago on her first day in Georgia. Feeling utterly alone, she'd run from the strange family she'd never known and hidden in an empty stall. They'd found her, coaxed her out, hugged her, soothed her, loved her.

She shivered.

Rachel touched her arm. "You okay?"

"Fine." She shrugged. "My aunt and uncle used to have a peanut farm in Georgia before they retired. Their stable was only half this size, though."

Muffled voices carried from the back where it was dark and shadowed. Jamie couldn't see anyone but she immediately recognized Cole's quiet husky drawl.

"I thought he'd left," Rachel said absently.

"Who?"

"Cole. He's supposed to be working on the irrigation system in the north pasture." Rachel picked up her pace. "Cole? Jesse?"

"Back here with Jezebel."

"Is she okay?" Rachel asked anxiously. "She's not due yet."

"She's fine…still pregnant."

The two men stepped out into the dappled sunlight sneaking in through a gap in the wall. Seeing Jamie, they lapsed into a brief uncomfortable silence.

She slowed behind Rachel. The brothers were of similar height and build, both had dark hair, but Cole's was longer. Still, they looked remarkably alike.

Rachel introduced Jesse, who was so cute he even took off his hat before he shook Jamie's hand.

"Nice to meet you, ma'am, but you'll have to excuse me," he said in a deep rumbling voice, and glanced at his sister. "I've got to make a run to the border to pick up a goat."

That startled a laugh out of Jamie.

"His date." Rachel grinned, and watched her brother shake his head as he headed out. "He works part-time as an animal rescue pilot."

"Wow." Jamie turned to watch him go. "How interesting."

Cole noisily cleared his throat. "I gotta be going, too."

Rachel caught his arm. "I thought you'd already left."

"I got sidetracked."

"Are you sure Jezebel's all right?"

He briefly glanced at Jamie, and she thought she saw a glint of guilt in his eyes. Maybe the brothers had been looking for a private place to talk. "Go see for yourself."

"Stay," Rachel said. "It's getting close to suppertime. Have a beer on the porch with our guests."

He frowned. "I got four hours of daylight left. I'll grab a sandwich when I get back."

"Come on, Cole, you work too hard."

Jamie couldn't see his face, but she could just imagine the glare he gave his sister as he strolled purposefully past her. "Mind if I go with you?" The words were out of Jamie's mouth before she considered them.

Even Rachel looked a bit stunned.

Jamie shrugged. "I've been cooped up in a plane or car all day. I wouldn't mind the fresh air."

Cole stared at her, looking as if he'd been cornered by a rattlesnake.

4

"I'M GOING OUT THERE to work. It won't be a pleasure ride," Cole said, looking to Rachel for help. He wasn't about to let Jamie go with him. Not only did he truly mean to replace those pipes that had been leaking, but he didn't need the distraction.

His sister thought for a moment. "How perfect," she said, giving him one of those determined looks that meant nothing but trouble. "That way we can expect you back at a decent hour."

Cole glared at the traitor, then realized Jamie was staring at him. He rolled his shoulder to ease the sudden kink of tension cramping his neck. "I think you'd be better off with Shane, one of our wranglers. He's been giving the guests riding lessons and—"

"I already know how to ride." Jamie met his eyes straight-on, giving not so much as a hint of what was going on in her head. She'd be a good poker player.

"Take Gypsy." Rachel ignored the pointed warning he sent her with the set of his mouth, and with sheer cussedness turned to Jamie. "She's that sweet bay mare in the first stall we passed."

Sighing, Cole took off his hat and plowed a hand through

his hair, then rubbed the back of his neck. "I don't mean to be contrary, but I'll say it plain. This isn't a good idea."

Her lips parted a little, her expression startled as if he'd splashed her with cold creek water, and then her long thick lashes swept the tops of her slightly flushed cheeks. "I'm sorry. You're right. I have no business pushing myself on you."

"You're not being pushy. It's just that you've got plenty of time for riding, and you haven't had a tour of the place yet."

Jamie smiled, moved a slim shoulder. "You're right, of course."

Ah, hell. Better that she would've played coy…that he could've ignored. But she seemed genuinely embarrassed, which made him feel like cow manure. "Hey, if you want a ride, I'll go saddle Gypsy for you," he murmured, and settled his hat back on his head.

"No, Cole, really…" Jamie caught his arm.

He froze, glanced down at the slim unadorned fingers curled around his forearm. A sudden warmth flooded his chest. The reaction puzzled him. A whole passel of females had been traipsing around the ranch for the past two weeks, a lot of them prettier than her.

She slowly withdrew her hand.

"Rachel, get her a hat to protect her face and eyes."

"I'm wearing sunscreen," Jamie said, already starting to back up. "I have a ball cap in the room. Won't take me but a minute to get it."

Something about her appealed to him. Or at least she didn't make him feel like hightailing it to the broken-down east line shack and holing up for the next week. Maybe it was her wide generous smile which seemed to come easily, or the fact that she had strong hands and sensible nails. He was a practical man. He appreciated those simple attributes in a woman.

He saw the soft heave of her high round breasts, looked into her clear hazel eyes and felt a smile tug at his mouth. She blinked, and he darted a look at his sister, who was staring at him as if he'd belched out loud in church. "What?"

As usual, Rachel wasn't fazed by his abruptness. "Nothing." She pressed her lips together, but that didn't stop the corners from twitching. "I have a hat for you, Jamie. Right over here."

Cole walked past them, his head down, wondering why the devil he'd given in. He wouldn't get any work done because he had every intention of taking Jamie for a short ride to the foothills and then turning around in time for her to drink her margarita and eat supper with the rest of the guests. Then he'd ride back out and finish his chores. And just maybe he'd bunk in the line shack after all.

"I've never been to Montana before. It's beautiful country." They'd reached the edge of the high mountain meadow dotted with orange and yellow wildflowers, and Jamie wished they could stop, just for a few minutes while she soaked in the beauty of the verdant landscape.

Cole didn't say a word. She hadn't expected him to, nor did she expect him to stop riding. He regretted letting her come with him—that much was clear from his stony silence during the twenty-five minutes they'd been riding.

"I checked out a map before I came. The western part of the state is flat. I don't think I'd like that much." She glanced over at him. "Is this all McAllister land?"

"Until the other side of the meadow."

She tugged down the borrowed brown hat, hoping to shade her eyes from the sinking sun, then squinted at the dense grove of pines climbing the mountainside. Any minute she was going to have to swallow her pride and ask him to stop. She wasn't a bad rider but it had been a while since she'd climbed on a horse, and ogling while staying in the saddle was becoming a bit too much. Plus she was getting stiff.

A minute later he reined in his beautiful chestnut gelding, and she wanted to throw her arms around him in gratitude. But then he'd probably send her back to the ranch. She figured the best way to show her appreciation for letting her tag along was to let him have his silence. So she listened to the wind rustle the aspen leaves and inhaled the crisp air, so fresh and clean it seemed almost unnatural.

"Your nose is pink."

"Oh." She touched the tip, momentarily self-conscious, unaware he'd been looking at her. "That always happens, even with sunscreen. Better than freckles, I suppose."

Their eyes met, briefly, before he found something on the side of the mountain to stare at, basically anything that wasn't her, while he lapsed again into silence. Fine. Maybe he'd already met his word quota for the day.

She seized the chance to study his profile, guessing that he was in his early thirties. She wasn't good at judging age to begin with, and the lines at the corners of his eyes, the groove in his cheek, all could be the result of working outdoors. Though whatever had conspired to create that face got two thumbs up from her. She liked what she saw, no doubt about that.

She didn't even mind that he wasn't talkative. He reminded her of the heroes in the old Westerns that she'd watched with her father. That her dad had been a sucker for a John Wayne or Gary Cooper yarn was the most human thing about him. Her mother would roll her eyes on that rare free night when he'd fix his martini, pop one of his beloved Westerns in the VHS player, and Jamie would cuddle with him on the couch, watching until she couldn't keep her eyes open.

Yeah, she liked thinking about Cole as one of those Western heroes. Tall, dark, quiet. He was perfect, sitting there looking sexy with that Stetson brim pulled low. All he needed was a gun belt and a rifle to complete the picture.

Nah, she wasn't fond of guns. Or God help her, the violent explosion of gunfire.

She closed her eyes, regretting that she'd invited the memory of that horrifying day so long ago, and lifted her face to the sun focusing on her breathing. While it had been too hot earlier, the warmth felt good now, especially with the slight breeze.

"You're a good rider."

She opened her eyes and looked at him. "Why the surprise?"

His lips moved a little, probably as close to a smile as she was going to get. "Most of the guests have been beginners."

"That has to be frustrating."

"They're my brother Trace's problem."

Jamie grinned.

"I didn't mean that like it sounded," he muttered, and squinted in the other direction.

She changed her mind. She didn't want him retreating into silence again. Distraction was better. "It's okay. I kind of get that the dude ranch thing was Rachel's idea." She paused. "I understand that some people around here aren't happy about the new business."

He turned his head sharply toward her. "Where did you hear that?"

"The gas station."

"Billy?" he asked, frowning.

"He was trying to explain Avery's attitude."

"Avery Phelps." Cole sighed and shook his head. "Nice welcome wagon."

"Billy was adorable. Avery not so much."

"What did the old man say to you?"

She shrugged. "I'm used to people like him. I make my living traveling. Wherever there are tourists, there will be Averys who don't want to share."

"It's not about sharing. It's about change. This is cattle country. Most folks around here want to keep it that way."

"What about you?"

His jaw tightened. "Just trying to make a living and take care of my family."

"You aren't married," she said too quickly, her gaze going to his hand even though she already knew he wore no ring.

"Nope."

"Ever been?"

His brown eyes warmed with amusement. "Why?"

She should've been embarrassed. She wasn't normally that blatantly inquisitive about a man. "I'm nosy."

"That could get you in trouble."

"Oh, it already has. Many times, actually. I haven't learned my lesson."

"I see that."

She liked that she'd almost made him smile. "So?"

"What?"

"Ever married? Or come close?"

He hesitated. "No."

Interesting that he'd had to think about it.

"What about you?"

She blinked, unprepared for him to turn the question around. "Not me," she said emphatically.

"Too busy traveling?"

She shrugged a shoulder and gave him a cheeky smile. "Nobody would have me."

"Right." Between his murmured drawl and the lingering gaze that slowly slid away from her body, a shiver raced down her spine.

She wondered if he was aware of the message he'd just sent. She hadn't imagined it. No way that heated look had been wishful thinking on her part. She breathed in deeply, then tried to swallow but her mouth was too dry.

"Ready to head back?" he asked.

"I thought you had work to do."

"Not up here," he said, lifting one brow in obvious amusement. "We irrigate the pasture when necessary."

"Then what are we doing here?"

"Thought you'd enjoy the view."

Damn the man. Here she'd thought they were making a little headway. "You figured I couldn't make the ride uphill and I'd beg you to take me back."

He lifted his Stetson then resettled it on his head, his gaze trained on the horizon. "You have a mighty suspicious mind."

She didn't trust the slow easy smile that curved his mouth. Sure, they'd go back to the Sundance, because she was about ready to kill for a beer or margarita, but he wasn't getting rid of her. Not this easily.

COLE DIDN'T KNOW what to make of Jamie. They hadn't spoken much on the ride back, and he liked that she was more comfortable with silence than any woman he'd ever met. She was different in other ways, too. Nothing he could pinpoint, because he didn't know her that well yet.

Hell, he wasn't planning on getting to know her better. No point in it. He wasn't *that* interested, and in six days she'd be gone, anyway. He'd made that mistake with his old girlfriend Bella after fooling himself into believing he knew her as well as a man could know a woman. The only thing positive he could say about the outcome was that he'd learned his lesson well. Luckily, he and Bella had worked out a comfortable arrangement and when she occasionally blew back into town for a couple of weeks, the sex was decent with no promises or expectations on either side.

So why was he thinking about Jamie Daniels at all? Why was he hanging around the west barn, catching glimpses of her mingling with the other guests, drinking margaritas and nibbling Hilda's homemade tortilla chips and salsa?

By the time he'd brushed down and watered Gypsy, he'd told himself it was too late to return to work. A damn lie for sure. With another two and a half hours of daylight left, he could've replaced three T-joints before he'd called it a day.

Hearing an engine, he ducked his head out to see the sheriff's white truck coming up the drive. Between the tinted windshield and the sun's glare, Cole couldn't tell if it was Noah or one of his deputies. Either way, this close to supper was an odd time for anyone to call.

He grabbed a rag to wipe his hands, and the sound of feminine laughter coming from the porch had him shaking his head. How could he have forgotten? The deputies were probably here to check out the new batch of guests who'd arrived today. Yep, he thought, sighing, the Sundance was starting to be a mighty busy place.

About to go back inside the barn, he was surprised to see Noah climb out of the truck. They'd been friends since before either one of them could tie their shoes, and Cole knew damn well Noah hadn't made a special trip to check out the women. He wore his customary jeans and tan uniform shirt. Had to still be working.

Noah spotted him, tugged down his brown Stetson, his attention on the gravel under his boots as he headed toward the barn.

"Hey, Sheriff Calder." Rachel called to him from the porch, waving to get his attention.

"Evenin', Rachel." Noah glanced her way, gave her a polite nod, then set his sights on Cole.

"Would you like to join us for a nice cold beer?"

"Thanks, but I'm on duty."

"We have iced tea," Rachel shouted. "Hilda made fresh salsa. Thick and spicy the way you like it."

Noah gave her a strained smile and a small shake of his head.

Chuckling, Cole watched a dozen women track his progress. A few were sitting on the rockers and the swing, but most of them stood at the railing, staring and showing their teeth. It might've looked like a Tupperware party except women around these parts tended not to run around half-naked, getting sunburned and wearing impractical high-heeled sandals.

As soon as Noah was close enough, he gestured with his eyes for them to meet inside the barn.

Try as he might to resist, Cole slid a parting glance toward Jamie. She wasn't watching Noah. Her gaze was on Cole. He pretended not to notice and waited inside.

His friend followed him with a scowl on his face.

"What? You don't like being eyed like a side of prime Angus?" Cole laughed at the hand gesture. "I heard they're partial to a man in uniform."

Noah snorted. "What the hell are you hanging around for? Didn't figure I'd catch you here."

Cole shrugged. "I took one of the new guests for a ride up to Big Jim Flats and just brought her back."

"You?" Noah's tanned face creased in surprise. "Which one?"

"What difference does it make?" Cole grabbed the pitchfork he'd been using and irritably stuck it in the hay. "It was a favor to Rachel."

"Could've sworn you said you were staying out of the business."

"You drove all the way out here to be a pain in my ass?"

Noah smiled, and from his position in the shadows of the barn door, ducked to get an undetected look at the porch. "I bet it was the blonde in the white shorts."

"Care to lay down a hundred on that?"

Noah eyed him with new interest, then went back to studying the assortment of ladies. "Can't be the one in the jeans."

Cole thought for a moment. Jamie was the only guest with the good sense to be wearing the appropriate clothes. "Where?"

"Right there. Dark blond hair. Real cute. Got a bum leg."

Cole shouldered his friend aside. Jamie's hair was dark

blond but there was nothing wrong with her leg. He would've noticed. "Who are you talking about?"

"She just sat down next to Rachel, but she's got a bad limp. Hope she didn't get hurt on your property."

"Jamie hadn't been limping," he murmured, half to himself. "Are you sure?"

"Jamie?"

Cole watched her grimace as she leaned over to take a beer off the tray Hilda had carried out. Rachel patted her arm with concern. Jamie shook her head, and gave a strained smile.

"Christ almighty." Cole sighed heavily. He understood the problem now, and he was mainly to blame.

Noah gave him a long measuring look. "What's wrong?"

The guy was more than a good friend, he was like a brother, but Cole wasn't in the mood to discuss Jamie with him, or anyone. Fortunately, Trace chose the perfect time to step out of the house and onto the porch. He'd changed into clean jeans and his hair was damp from a shower.

Snorting, Cole motioned with his chin. "Look at that."

Noah chuckled. "Maybe you can get stud fees for the kid."

"That's a thought." Cole grunted. "Hell, might be the only way I'd get a decent day's work out of him. Ever since the women got here he's been doing nothing but preening like a rooster."

They both watched Trace shamelessly flirt with the guests. The women swarmed to him like hummingbirds to nectar. Not Jamie, though. She stayed where she was, talking to Rachel, occasionally laughing at something someone said. When she glanced toward the barn, Cole turned away.

"You really on duty?" he asked Noah.

"Yeah." Noah took off his hat and slapped it against the front of his thigh sending dust particles in the air. "Got a call from Mrs. Clements. Claims someone stole one of her four-wheelers."

"Can't be right." There hadn't been a theft in Salinas

County for as long as Cole could recall. "The old woman has so much junk on her property, she probably misplaced it."

"That's my way of thinking. Naturally Avery had to stick his nose in, jabbering on about how this is what happens when you bring in outsiders."

Cole stared at his friend. "You think one of the… Is that why you're here?"

"You know me better than that, McAllister." Noah sighed. "I figured I'd ask around, see if anyone's noticed if things have gone missing."

He shook his head. "The men would've mentioned it."

"I expect it'll turn out to be nothing, just like you said, probably misplaced. But the truth is, these are hard times. We don't like to think our neighbors would resort to stealing, but a lot of men are out of work and they've got kids to feed. They see an elderly widow hoarding stuff she doesn't use—" Noah shrugged, his expression grim. "Who's to say…?"

Cole studied his friend. Unlike Cole, Noah had left long enough to serve in the army and go to college, then work as a big-city cop for a few years before deciding to return to Blackfoot Falls. He'd seen the ugly side of humanity. In Noah's line of work, Cole understood it was good not to be too trusting. Sadly, even of their own neighbors.

"As much as I was against this dude ranch idea of Rachel's, between you and me, it's bringing in a nice piece of change."

"Hey, you do what you gotta do." Noah set his hat back on his head. "I had breakfast at Marge's this morning and the folks sitting at the counter were talking about maybe starting their own guest ranches."

"Avery would have a conniption. Hell, I wouldn't be so thrilled myself."

Noah chuckled. "Trace would think he'd died and gone to heaven."

Whatever he'd meant to say to Noah slipped clean out of Cole's mind as his gaze got snagged on a piercing stare from the only guest he gave a damn about. *Hello, trouble,* he thought, as he fought to keep his expression neutral when his body had ideas that were anything but.

5

As disgusted as she was to be confined to her room her first night at the Sundance, Jamie knew damn well she deserved to be sidelined. She hadn't ridden a horse in years, and while she'd known she was skilled enough to keep up with Cole, her aching body was calling her every kind of stupid.

She was in fairly good shape from routine exercise and some hiking, but straddling a horse strained a unique and seldom-used set of muscles.

Idiotic pride, that's all it was. Cole had expected a city girl who couldn't keep up and she'd wanted to show him....

Yeah, right. Really smart.

She twisted toward the nightstand to reach her glass of iced tea. Pain knifed her hip.

"Ouch." She added a curse for good measure, then shifted her laptop to the side while she found a more comfortable position on the queen-size bed.

At least she was starting off with some good material for her blog, she thought wryly. Her readers would find this pretty funny. Though she wouldn't post it for another six days. No way Jamie wanted Cole to know how foolish she'd been to ride for so long. After she was gone, he could laugh all he wanted.

Speaking of being a fool, she shifted just enough for a sharp stabbing pain to work its way up her thigh. "Oh, God," she moaned. Did this mean sex was out of the question?

She sat up straighter to ease the cramp and groaned so loudly she almost missed the knock on the bedroom door. Had to be Rachel with more dessert. As if that would fix everything.

Seriously tempted to tell her to go away, Jamie sighed, then said, "Come in."

"It's Cole."

"Oh." She touched her hair and unsuccessfully glanced around for a mirror. Knowing she looked like crap, she swung her legs off the bed. Her muscles screamed in agony. It wasn't worth moving.

"If you're not decent then I can—"

"It's okay." She grinned. Did guys really say stuff like that? Apparently so. "Come in." She tugged down the hem of her shorts to avoid a camel-toe but the gesture gave her an idea. Quickly she unfastened the top two buttons of her blouse. There. That should distract him.

The door slowly opened. He stood hesitantly at the threshold, his broad shoulders stretching across an impressive amount of space. His hat was gone, his hair combed back, and he'd changed into a snug black T-shirt and dark slim-fitting jeans. He still wore boots, and damn, he looked good. This surprise visit was so going into her blog.

Unless this pop-in turned into something juicy....

She tried to move closer to the edge of the bed without bawling like a five-year-old.

"Don't," he said, his worried gaze going to her bare legs. The concern in his eyes told her that Rachel had blown the whistle. "I'm not staying. I brought you something."

Jamie darted a look at his hand, but she couldn't see what he was holding. "It's nothing, honestly—" she murmured, distracted by the strange pattern of pale scars that lashed the back of his hand. They looked old, and she might have missed them if he weren't so tanned.

"I'm also here to apologize." He gave his head a shake of self-recrimination.

"You think this is your fault?"

"Of course it's my fault. I should've asked when you were in a saddle last."

She grinned. "You're adorable, you know that?"

He frowned, and to clinch his adorable status, a flush crept up his neck.

Jamie inched her butt closer to the edge of the bed, grimacing, as if that helped. "I knew better than to ride for that long a period of time after not being on a horse in so many years."

"Still, I shouldn't have let you—"

"*Let* me? I'm not a child."

"No, but you were my responsibility."

She laughed. "I haven't been anyone's responsibility for a helluva long time, thank you very much."

Cole blinked, his expression mildly surprised, and then that stubborn glint was back in his eyes, the look she'd seen earlier. Made her wonder if he was the kind of guy who took the big-brother thing way too seriously. There was no father in the picture as far as she could tell.

"Help me up," she said, "please."

Without hesitation he offered his hand. Across his palm were more scars. Startled, she looked away to keep from staring, and let him gently pull her to her feet.

God, she wanted to ask what had happened to him, but now didn't seem like the right time. She wanted him to keep holding her hand, the rough scarred skin feeling oddly exciting against her palm. For a second she tried to imagine how it would feel against the softer skin of her breasts.

She cleared her throat and glanced at the small jar he'd switched to his other hand. "What's that?"

"Some liniment that should help."

"Rachel already gave me something."

"This is better."

With some effort, Jamie straightened and watched him set the unmarked jar on the bedside table. He hadn't let go of her hand yet, and that was fine with her. "Not that I don't trust you, but why didn't Rachel give me that in the first place?"

"Probably because it stinks like hell."

"Ah. A homemade remedy, I take it."

"It's something the Blackfoot use."

She tilted her head back to gaze up at him. His brown eyes shouldn't have been anything unusual, except they were. No gold or amber flecks to distinguish them, but somehow they stirred a need inside her to find out what lurked behind his carefully passive gaze.

Before she realized she was going to touch him, she reached up and ran the pad of her thumb over his high strong cheekbones. "Do the McAllisters have some Native American blood?"

Surprise flickered in his eyes, but he didn't even flinch. "Nothing I can prove."

"You boys all have dark hair and eyes, but then Rachel is so fair like your mother."

His hand closed a bit more tightly around hers. "Trace has green eyes."

"Does he?"

Cole smiled. "He'd be offended that you didn't notice."

"Then we won't tell him." She smiled back, thinking about how the rest of the women had fluttered around Trace earlier. Sure, he was a cutie and charming as hell, but something about Cole's reluctant smile and the way his left brow seemed to lift at will made her toes curl.

She was still touching his face. For no reason. Other than that she liked it, and she'd started to hope it would lead to a kiss. "Thanks," she said, finally forcing herself to lower her hand.

"I wager it doesn't feel like it, but you're doing the right thing by moving around." He released her, too, and stepped back to give her room.

"I know. Tonight humiliation won out. Tomorrow I'll walk out some of this stiffness."

"Better if you do it now."

Her gaze went to the window, even though she'd already drawn the drapes. "It's dark."

"There's a full moon, no clouds." He shrugged. "I'll take you for a stroll if you'd like."

A walk in the moonlight with Cole? She had to think about it…for at least half a second. "Uh, yeah, that would be great. If I'm not putting you out."

"Nope."

She glanced down at her shorts. She never wore them outdoors but sometimes slept in them. They didn't leave much to the imagination. "Should I change?"

"No need."

The painful thought of trying to yank on jeans made her shudder. These would have to do. Besides, the way some of the other women had dressed for drinks and dinner, one would've thought they were vacationing on a beach.

"You might want to take care of that, though," Cole said in that low husky drawl of his.

She looked at him, saw him shooting uneasy glances at her chest. Ah. Her buttons. She'd forgotten that she'd unfastened them. Both flaps of her yellow Henley top lay back, forming a V that exposed a wedge of cream-colored lace and more cleavage than she could truthfully claim, thanks to her uplift bra. Talk about false advertising.

"Ah, right." She pulled the flaps together. "I should change."

"Not on my account."

"I don't want to make you uncomfortable." Buttoned, the top was fine. It was the brief shorts…

Cole chuckled. "Honey, if it were up to me..." He trailed off, shaking his head, his expression part-irritated, part-amused. "How about I wait for you outside?"

"No. Wait. What were you going to say?" she asked, grinning, excitement fluttering in her belly.

"Just poking fun at myself." He moved to the door, the faintest trace of a smile tugging at his mouth.

"Come on."

"Take your time. I'll be out front." He grabbed the door-knob.

"You big fat yellow-bellied chicken."

"Yes, ma'am," he said with a polite nod as he opened the door.

"Don't leave me to hobble out there by myself. I'm going to need help."

His dry look told her that he knew she was totally lying. Okay, so she might not need his help but she did want him to walk out with her. She'd seen Tammy and Lynn, the two brunettes from Chicago, giving him the onceover, and heard their remarks. Better the pair of vultures saw that she had first dibs on him.

"Please, Cole." She limped pathetically toward him.

His gaze went down her legs. "Shoes?"

"Oh, yeah, that would help." The thought of bending over and pulling on her running shoes made her want to weep. Maybe the walk wasn't worth it. She could stay in her room and groan in peace through a few stretching exercises.

He found her shoes stashed beside the dresser and then motioned with his chin toward the bed.

"What?"

"Sit," he ordered, obviously mistaking her hesitation for confusion, and held out his hand to her.

She frowned, curious and oddly turned on as she let him steady her to a perch at the edge of the bed.

He crouched down, scooped her heel into the palm of his

large hand and set her foot on his knee. She clenched her teeth together to keep from bloodying her lower lip, wishing she wore a dainty size-six shoe instead of a big honking nine. Still, she'd gotten a pedicure a week ago so that was something to be thankful for. Plus the socks he'd grabbed were clean.

She watched him slide the white socks over her polished pink toenails, over her foot, his hands incredibly gentle as he tugged the band snugly in place around her ankle. He carefully kept his eyes on his task, not once letting his gaze wander up her leg, his cautious avoidance telling her more than he'd probably appreciate her interpreting.

Not that she was a paragon of logic at the moment. The whole thing was crazy. Watching him switch to the other foot, she tried to keep still, tried not to think about her tightened nipples or how insanely intimate this seemed.

Jamie's only one-night stand, hours after Kaylee had stood at that altar and said "I do," hadn't come close to the intimacy of Cole slipping on her socks. For her, anyway. All this stuff going full-speed in her head, and he probably wasn't giving any of it a second thought.

He finished making sure her shoes were on and tied, and finally met her eyes as he pushed up to a standing position. His dilated pupils made her breathing stutter. He put out his hand and she took it, his skin warm against her cool damp palm.

Men didn't normally throw her off balance like this. She lowered her gaze, not crazy about the idea of not being fully in control. On the other hand, those were some mesmerizing dark eyes.

She smiled. "Ready?"

"Give me a minute. I have to stop by my room."

"Shall I wait here?"

"Up to you. I'm right next door."

"Oh." She tried to look cool, but hot damn.

COLE LEFT HER IN THE HALL while he ducked inside. It shouldn't matter that her room was next to his. It wasn't as though he walked or talked in his sleep, but he didn't like her being so close, sharing a wall with him.

So why the hell was he going for a walk with her? He'd been around long enough to know that from some women a man simply needed to keep his distance. Sometimes you understood why—the reason was as plain as a mare in heat—and sometimes you couldn't nail down the problem, you just knew.

Jamie Daniels fell into the latter category.

He headed straight for the attached bathroom, turned on the faucet and splashed cold water on his face. A quick walk once around the house and maybe the stables. Then he'd bring her back, part company with her at the bottom of the stairs. She'd come up to her room, and he'd go to the study and clear some paperwork. No big deal.

After drying his face, he used some mouthwash and stared at himself in the mirror. One thing was for certain, he was too damn old to be having that jittery feeling in his gut knowing it was going to be just Jamie and him in the moonlight.

Hell, he was just horny. Bella hadn't been in town for a while, and in a small place like Blackfoot Falls, he pretty much knew every woman over eighteen. He couldn't see himself getting serious with any of them, but he could get in a whole lot of trouble if he were stupid enough to ask a local woman out on more than three dates. Inevitably she'd get the wrong idea and then there would be hurt feelings and too much gossip. That was the good thing about living in a city, Noah had told him. Women there weren't quick to think marriage. Some good sex…until it wasn't good anymore…and then everyone went on with their lives. Of course there were exceptions, but it wasn't as if you had a whole town following your every move.

He'd bet his boots Jamie could be one of those level-headed

women. Problem was, he'd warned the men to watch themselves around the guests, and wouldn't it be something if he were the one to set a precedent?

Nah. Knowing Trace, he'd probably already done that honor. Cole tossed the hand towel on the rack and fingercombed his hair. Past due for a trim. Maybe he'd make the time to run into town and visit Sherman tomorrow. The barber would be surprised to see him. Cole had been letting Hilda whack at his hair when he couldn't stand it sticking to the back of his neck. But she was busier now with all the guests to cook for and clean up after. He wouldn't bother her.

He'd only been gone a minute but Jamie wasn't in the hall where he'd left her. She stood at the top of the staircase, staring out the front window at the moon. It was something to see, all right—big and full, shining with an otherworldly glow.

Times like this made him glad he'd been stubborn about putting in that window.

Folks in town had thought he was nuts when he'd started the project. They'd been quick to point out that if he wanted to watch the sun set or the moon rise, all he had to do was step outside. Then the hands had teased him mercilessly about being a sappy romantic. Hell, that had nothing to do with it. He'd figured it was a shame to shut out that kind of beauty. No harm in letting creation in.

Jamie looked over as he approached. "I have never seen a moon like this. Not even in Tahiti or Fiji where the light pollution is low." She turned back to the window. "This is incredible. I feel as though I can reach out and touch it."

He was foolishly pleased with her reaction. As if he'd had something to do with the damn moon. They stared out in silence for a few moments, and then she smiled at him, giving him a long enough look that he wondered if he should've used a real comb on his hair.

Laughter drifted up from the great room, and Jamie blinked. "Ready if you are," she said softly.

He nodded, gestured for her to go first. But the staircase was wide enough that they fell into step abreast of each other and, by tacit agreement, remained quiet until they were out the front door, no one the wiser.

The moonlight was enough. No need for artificial light, even though some of it flooded out of the east barn and the bunkhouse. Cole steered her to the right, where there would be less chance of running into anyone. The issue wasn't so much about wanting her alone as it was about the men getting the wrong idea.

He glanced down at her profile—the slightly upturned nose, the long thick lashes, the curve of her pink lips as she gazed up at the sky. She hadn't said a single word since the top of the stairs. He couldn't recall a woman so unhurried to fill the silence with frivolous chatter.

Hell, maybe it wasn't so bad wanting her to himself for a while. She wasn't just pretty, she was smart and easygoing, sensible…except for insisting on riding too long.

"How's the stiffness?" he asked.

"Not bad, really. I think I bruised my pride more than anything else."

Cole smiled. "The ointment won't help with that."

"Oh, my God, that ointment." She made a face. "I took a whiff of that stuff while you were in your room. The pain might be preferable."

"Might want to think again. Keeps away rattlers, too."

"I wouldn't doubt it," she said, then stopped. "Are there snakes around here?"

"Not where you'll be stepping." He touched the small of her back, and she drew closer.

He wasn't sure what to do about that new development. He hadn't meant anything except to reassure her. But he couldn't say he minded her nearness….

Or when she slipped an arm through his and peered up at

him. "Do you mind?" she asked, her eyes wide and questioning. "The air's a bit cooler than I expected."

"It's the altitude. Once the sun goes down…" Damn, he should've known better. He was okay in a T-shirt, but he wished he had something to offer for around her shoulders. "Did you want to go back inside?"

"No," she said quickly. "It feels good after today's heat. I'm just surprised."

He felt a little awkward, not knowing if he should tug her closer and share his heat or leave well enough alone. Problem was, his body had reacted to the sweet feminine scent of her skin and the soft warmth of her breast nestled against his arm.

She must've felt his tension because she started to pull away.

He closed a hand over hers and tightened his arm. "I don't mind," he said, and heard her breathy sigh. "But you let me know when you wanna turn around."

"I love it out here." She looked up at the sky as they started to walk again. "So many stars. It's beautiful. I'd like to camp out one night if that's possible. Guess I need to talk to Rachel about that."

"Where are you from?"

Jamie grinned, her teeth gleaming. "That's tricky. I've lived in a lot of different places."

"Where do you live now?"

"Southern California is home base. West L.A. to be exact, though I spend only half my time there."

He'd never been to California but he'd heard enough about it that he doubted most women from there were like Jamie. "Where did you learn to ride?"

"My aunt and uncle's peanut farm in Georgia. I was nine, but I've ridden on and off over the years." She stopped and swung around to face him. "Take me camping for a night."

Floored, he just stared at her.

"Please," she whispered, tilting her head back and meeting his eyes before her gaze settled on his mouth.

His heart thundered in his chest. She looked so pretty with the moon glowing in her face. He wanted to kiss her, and he was pretty damn sure she wanted the same thing.

He lowered his head, and she lifted up the rest of the way to meet him. He brushed his lips across her petal-soft ones, and felt the small tremor in the hand she'd pressed to his chest.

A wheezing laugh slid into a cough, breaking the stillness of the night. They automatically jumped apart, and Cole noticed a dark figure leaning against the corral fence.

"Wouldn't have believed it if I hadn't seen it with my own eyes. The great Cole McAllister has finally been knocked off his high horse." A bottle of whiskey in hand, Wallace Gunderson moved into the light. "I see you'd rather whore yourself out than sell me a damn speck of land."

6

COLE COULD BARELY contain his anger. He pulled away from Jamie and moved closer to Gunderson, who staggered sideways. No way he'd take a swing at the older man, though not because he wasn't tempted. "What the hell are you doing here?"

Wallace smiled, tipped the bottle of whiskey to his lips, then used the back of his sleeve to wipe his mouth. "I wonder what your daddy would think of this pitiful predicament of yours, the way you've run this fine ranch into the ground."

"I strongly suggest you leave of your own accord," Cole warned in a low, controlled voice. Inside he shook with rage. Normally he wouldn't give a damn what the stupid bastard had to say. He was clearly drunk, and he always spouted off when he had too much liquor in him. But that Jamie had heard…

"Or what?" Gunderson cackled, swayed from side to side then squinted at Jamie. "Have some manners, boy. Introduce me to this fine-looking gal."

"I'm not telling you again, Gunderson."

Wallace moved closer. "I saw your surveyor out there a couple months back. He was tagging the strip that backs up to government land, so I know you been considering selling off a parcel. But I ain't interested in that piece, so you can keep it." He belched loudly. "You know damn well which section I want, boy."

It took just about all of Cole's willpower not to pick the man up by the back of his shirt, toss him into the barn and lock him in there till morning came or he sobered up. Cole looked over at Jamie. "You mind going back to the house on your own?"

"Yes, I do." She glared at Gunderson. "I don't appreciate being interrupted by a man who's clearly old enough to know better than to get publicly drunk and act like a common bully."

The man stared at her for a second, then started laughing again, lapsing into the vile rusty wheezing. "You got yourself a spirited filly there, McAllister." He jerked his chin toward the house. "I just might have me a look at the rest of the fresh mares you got stabled."

When he took an unsteady step toward the house, Cole didn't have much of a choice but to get in Gunderson's face, but Jamie caught Cole's arm.

"I know you're trying to help," he told her tightly, "but you need to stay out of this."

The door from the bunkhouse opened, and laughter and lights flooded the night. Kyle and Josh, two of the younger hands, walked toward Josh's ancient pickup, grousing about a poker game they'd obviously just left.

They stopped when they spotted Cole and Gunderson.

"Hey, Cole," Kyle said uncertainly, his gaze shooting to the old man, and then to Jamie. "We were just headed to town… unless you need us for something."

"I think Mr. Gunderson could use a ride home," Cole said quietly. "If you boys don't mind."

From the dread expression on their faces they minded plenty. The man had no fans clear to the Canadian border, but Josh shrugged, shook his head. "Nah, no problem, boss."

"I ain't ready to leave yet." Gunderson's words were even more slurred than they had been minutes ago. "Got my own damn truck, anyway."

"You either accept a ride from the boys here, or you can wait while I call the sheriff," Cole said, unable to resist a small smile, his threat clear. "I'm pretty sure Noah wouldn't mind giving you a lift to town where you can sleep it off."

Gunderson swayed back and forth, his fists clenching. "You're nothing but a goddamn smart-ass, McAllister. Cut from the same cloth as your hardheaded old man."

"Come on, Mr. Gunderson. Lucas can follow us in your truck." Josh approached the older man, easily ducking when Gunderson took a sloppy swing at him.

The effort nearly sent Gunderson sprawling face-forward in the dirt, but Josh, a tall, husky ex-high-school linebacker, smoothly caught the man around the waist and hoisted him over his shoulder.

Gunderson let out a string of profanities but settled down after a quiet warning from Josh—who was a good kid, but he'd never been known to back down from a fight.

Cole picked up the whiskey bottle that had landed perilously close to Jamie's feet, a fact that made him want to throw a punch himself. "Make sure he gets in the house, then hide his truck keys. He can call and find out where they are tomorrow."

"You got it, boss." Josh effortlessly carried the limp drunk toward his truck.

Cole was pretty sure Gunderson had passed out and hoped so for the boys' sake, or he was likely to give them a hard time for the twenty-minute ride to his place. Reluctant to face Jamie, Cole silently watched until both trucks pulled onto the driveway.

The humiliation of Gunderson's accusation still burning in his belly, he heaved a defeated sigh. "Sorry you had to witness that."

"I'm sorry you have such an ass for a neighbor." She paused. "Are you mad at me?"

He turned to look at her. "Of course not."

"You'd have every right. I shouldn't have butted in, but I didn't want him ruining our evening."

He looked away. She wanted him to tell her everything was all right, they could act as if nothing had happened. He wished it were that easy. What Gunderson had said…what Jamie had seen and heard… Hell, Cole might as well have been stripped naked and paraded down Main Street. "I'll walk you back."

"Why? It's early."

"Jamie, I'm sorry."

She laid a hand on his arm. "He was drunk," she said, then quickly added, "Though I'm in no way defending him. What I'm doing a bad job of saying is that I haven't given what he said a second thought…if that's the problem."

Cole breathed in deeply and stared at the sky. Funny how only fifteen minutes ago there seemed to have been a whole different moon up there. And the stars…not so bright anymore. "I've gotta get up early tomorrow. If you wanna keep walking, stick to the area near the corral fence, around the barn and the house. You'll be safe. You might hear coyotes but they won't come down this close."

"Coyotes?" She withdrew her hand. "Maybe one of the men in the bunkhouse wouldn't mind escorting me around the property," she said sweetly.

His instant aversion to the idea of one those young bucks strolling with Jamie in the moonlight shocked him. Everything from the way his gut clenched to the tightness of his chest worsened his mood. "I suspect any number of them would be happy to oblige."

She let out an unladylike snort. "I don't want anyone else. I want you."

He scrubbed a hand over his face. If he couldn't admit to himself that he was pleased by her words he'd be a liar. Didn't change anything though. What Gunderson had said cut too deep. McAllisters were ranchers, not hotelmen or anything else. But to accuse him of whoring himself out. Shit.

"You're really going to ditch me, aren't you?"

Cole said nothing.

"This isn't fair."

"Nope," he said quietly. "I don't expect it is."

"You don't even know what I'm talking about."

He almost smiled, despite the fact he suddenly felt so damn drained, as if he hadn't slept for a week. Come to think of it, when was his last decent night's sleep? "Take your pick. Every part of tonight qualifies."

"Fine. Go hide in the house. Let the bastard win." She gasped softly. "Sorry. I shouldn't have said that."

Cole squinted in the direction of the driveway. Both trucks were long gone. But the sour echo of Gunderson's words lingered heavily in the air, dimming the magical glow of the moon. He didn't particularly want to disappoint her. In another life, she'd be someone he'd want to know well, but it was neither the time nor the place. "Good night, Jamie. Use the liniment. You'll feel better tomorrow."

She'd waited until he'd made it a few yards, and asked, "Will I see you?"

He knew what she meant, but the answer she got was, "You're here for another six days. I reckon you will."

"HOLD IT." RACHEL SHUFFLED into the kitchen just as Cole was headed for the back door, a to-go mug of steaming black coffee in hand.

Dammit. He'd figured he'd be halfway to Pine Meadow before anyone stirred. "What are you doing up this early?"

She covered a yawn, then cinched the belt of her robe. "Trying to catch you before you sneak out."

"Sneak out? You've been living in the city too long," he said irritably. "Work starts at sunup."

She grunted, yawning again as she opened the upper oak cupboard and got a mug. "Sit with me for a minute."

He considered making up an excuse because he was pretty sure he knew this was about Jamie and last night, but no sense delaying the inevitable. While she dumped sugar and cream into her coffee, he pulled out a chair at the kitchen table, sat down and glanced at the round wall clock. He'd give her five minutes.

With his booted foot, he pushed out the chair across from him, and Rachel sat down. "I'll get right to it. Jamie wants to hang out with you."

Cole sipped. They needn't have bothered sitting down. "No."

"No?" She narrowed her gaze. "Just like that. No?"

"What did I tell you from the beginning?"

"Oh, God, you're as bullheaded as Pop was." She took a long sip of coffee and sighed. "I thought you got on okay with her, that maybe you even liked her a little."

"I like her fine."

"So what's the big deal?" She glanced at the door, then lowered her voice. "She isn't like some of those other women. She doesn't giggle and she knows which end of a horse to feed. I think she's genuinely interested in the workings of a ranch. And I'm not kidding about how much great advertising we'd get if she has a good time."

Puzzled, he stared at his sister. It wasn't like her not to bring up the incident with Gunderson right off the top. "When did Jamie ask you about this?"

"Last night." She shrugged. "Right before bedtime. She'd been out for a walk."

"I know." He smiled to himself. So she hadn't said anything to Rachel about what had happened. "She was with me."

Rachel's eyes widened. "Tell me."

"Tell you what?"

"Everything."

Cole laughed and shook his head. Right now she looked just like she had when she was twelve. "Jamie was stiff from riding and I told her she'd be better off walking and stretching those sore muscles.... What?"

Rachel was smiling so hard he thought her face might break.

"I gotta get moving." He pushed back from the table, thought twice about taking the time to refill his coffee. But then, what the hell—he needed the caffeine and he had nothing to hide. She could grin as much as she damn wanted.

He poured more of the strong dark brew that he'd made to his liking. "By the way, I take it she didn't say anything about Gunderson."

Rachel lost her smile. "Wallace Gunderson?" Her brows dipped. "Why would she? How would she know him?"

"He was here last night."

"Oh, my God. I hope none of the guests... Was he drunk?"

"He'd been tipping the bottle all right."

"What happened?" Rachel asked, the dread in her voice as thick as Hilda's country gravy.

Cole slid a gaze to the window. It was already light, but he figured he might as well say something before the hands started talking. "Same as always. He still wants that creek land. Guess he was hoping we were finally desperate enough to take his cash."

"So he's pissed about us opening the dude ranch...." She rubbed her right temple. "All of it in front of Jamie. Dammit. Do I want to know the specifics?"

"No point in it." Thinking about Gunderson and last night's scene made his blood boil all over again. "Jamie got in her two cents, though—handed him a good dressing-down for interrupting our walk."

Rachel gave him a measuring look long enough to make him itch to leave. "I hate that she had to hear a single word out of that vile man's mouth, but I hate it even more that it happened in front of you."

He shrugged. "At least I didn't punch the old bastard. I sure as hell wanted to."

She nodded absently. "Jamie didn't say a word. Pretty classy. Still, I'll apologize to her."

"I'd leave it be." He wished he could. Replaying the incident had kept him up a good two hours longer than he'd liked. "Gunderson will be calling later to find out where Josh and Lucas hid his keys. They drove him home."

Rachel winced. "That drunk, huh? Wait, don't go yet."

He reluctantly stopped at the door. "Nothing left to talk about."

"The Jamie issue?"

"I gave you my answer."

"Look, now that I know about last night, I understand why you're embarrassed but—"

"That's got nothing to do with why I'm not letting her follow me around. I'm too busy getting ready for the Missoula auction and fall roundup. You know that."

"Sure." She sniffed. "No one can ever accuse me of not doing *my* part to keep this ranch afloat."

"That's a fact," he said, ignoring her taunt and then made it out the kitchen door before her glare burned a hole in his back.

WALKING INTO ABE'S VARIETY STORE gave Cole little reprieve from the heat. Though when he saw the door propped open he knew beforehand that the fans would be going instead of the air-conditioning. No one complained about Abe wanting to save a few bucks. His customers were glad he'd managed to stay open this long and continue to offer his dusty merchandise.

"I had two of 'em stop at the diner. Real nice gals, except they tried to order some strange sandwich I never heard of. Something with alfalfa sprouts. I told 'em we feed those things to the horses." Marge laughed along with Louise, who owned the fabric shop next door.

Abe shook his head, a smile on his ruddy face as he rang up Marge's purchase. "I hope they all start coming to town more. I sold a few tubes of lip balm and they wiped me out of my sunblock, but I'm thinking of ordering some souvenir items from Glacier Falls."

"One of them came into my place and asked if I sold ready-made Western shirts," Louise said, her normally rusty voice sounding excited. "Told her I could sew one up before she left, but she seemed disappointed. Said she'd let me know later. I figured I'd talk to Barbara, see how many more guests they're expecting this year before I bring in some ready-mades."

Abe passed Marge her package and spotted Cole. "There's the man to ask."

The two older women turned and gave him friendly smiles. He'd known Marge since he was old enough to walk. Her hair had always been big, only now it was gray, and he was fairly certain she even slept with her lips painted that bright red.

"What about it, handsome?" Marge asked. "You all booked up through fall out there at the Sundance?"

"You'll have to talk to Rachel. I'm staying out of that side of things." He would've avoided Blackfoot Falls if he could, at least for another couple of weeks until the excitement and gossip died down, but he'd agreed to attend the last-minute town meeting that had been called to discuss some issues on water rights.

"You heard about Mrs. Clements's missing four-wheeler?" Abe asked.

"'Course I did." Cole scooped a pound bag of rope licorice from a basket sitting at the end of the counter. "Anybody in the county *not* hear about it?"

Abe chuckled. "Good point."

"That damn-fool woman." Louise clucked her tongue. "Both her and Avery. Trying to make folks believe your guests had something to do with it. Like they don't have everything provided for them at the Sundance."

Marge glanced over her shoulder. "Keep your voice down. We don't want those girls showing up and overhearing. To my way of thinking, we're lucky to have their business."

"Amen." Louise nodded solemnly. "Just last month Sylvie and me were considering it might be smart to close up shop for a while. Now with tourists coming to town, maybe we can actually come out a few pennies ahead."

"Don't let Avery hear that kind of talk." Abe's mouth twitched with amusement. He'd never minded stirring up a little trouble now and again. "He's been on the warpath over this dude ranch business. No offense to you and yours," he said, glancing at Cole.

"The hell with that old coot," Marge said. "Fine for him to be shooting his mouth off. Both him and Mrs. Clements have enough money squirreled under their mattresses to carry them through a hundred-year drought."

"Bite your tongue, woman." Abe frowned. *Drought* was a curse word around Salinas County.

Anxious to be on his way and avoid talk of the Sundance, Cole laid the licorice on the counter, added a package of breath mints, then dug in his jeans pocket for some cash.

While Abe rang up his purchase on a register that was older than Cole, Marge picked up the mints and studied the package as if she didn't know what they were. Then she grinned at him. "Guess one of them gals picked you out of the lineup. Can't say I'm surprised."

Leave it to Marge to try and make a connection between breath mints and a woman. Hell, it wasn't as if he'd never bought them before. Even when Bella wasn't in town.

Louise muffled a coarse chuckle. "That sister of yours is a very smart girl. Maybe I should ask her to do me up one of those fancy websites."

"Except you don't have any young handsome brothers to use as bait." Marge handed him the mints and winked.

He wondered what the hell they were talking about, but he knew better than to ask. "Abe, ladies…" He nodded. "I'll see you all later."

"I hope so." Marge raised her voice so that it followed him to the door. "Don't you McAllister boys go hogging those women. We could use their business."

The words had barely left Marge's mouth when Cole came face to face with Jamie. She'd come from out of nowhere, through the open door as he tried to escape. His arms automatically went up, and he caught her by her shoulders to avoid a collision.

"Cole." She pressed her palms lightly to his chest and reared her head, her eyes wide. "What are you doing here?"

Behind her was another Sundance guest, a blonde he recognized but not by name. She smiled at him, gave Jamie a startled look, then swung her curious gaze back to Cole.

He released Jamie's shoulders and stepped back. "I'm in town for a meeting."

"Ah." She slid her hands down to his belly, her fingers grazing his belt buckle before breaking contact. He did everything in his power to keep from reacting like a horny fifteen-year-old boy. "I thought you rode out early to avoid me," she said, her pretty pink lips tilting up at the corners.

"I did." He moved to the side so they could enter the store. "Ride out early." Hell, he could practically feel Marge's nosy breath on the back of his neck. "How's the stiffness?"

"Better. You were right about me staying in motion. The walk last night helped."

"I'm Brenda, by the way." The blonde stuck out her hand. "I know you're Cole. I saw you a couple times at the Sundance, but we've never met."

"Ma'am." He touched the brim of his hat, but she was intent on shaking hands, so he obliged her, then abruptly pulled back when he saw the frank challenge sparkling in her blue eyes. These city women were really something. At least they didn't keep a man guessing. "Got to get going. Can't be late for the meeting."

"Can we talk later?" Jamie asked in a rush when she clearly realized that he meant business about leaving. "When you get back to the ranch."

To answer truthfully would get him in more trouble than he wanted, what with Louise and Marge's ears perked up like wolfhounds. "Sure. Don't know what time that'll be, though."

"Anytime is fine. I'm not doing much today."

"See you when I get back, then." This time he hurried off with purpose, cringing when he overheard Brenda call him cute, followed by Marge's cackling laugh.

7

On her way to the den to join the other guests, Jamie glanced out the window and saw the dust, about half a mile down the driveway. Seconds later a black pickup emerged, headed toward the house, and she knew it was Cole. Finally.

She'd returned from town at about two-thirty and until giving up an hour ago, she'd been keeping an eye out for him. Had he made it in time for margaritas and beer on the porch, she would've been shocked. He didn't like mingling with the guests, and though Rachel had said nothing, Jamie guessed he'd shot down the idea of her tagging along with him for the rest of the week.

After dinner, Rachel had tried to talk her into signing up for a white-water rafting trip tomorrow. Trace and Liam, a cute young wrangler with sandy-blond hair and a shy smile, were organizing the outing and the women had been all abuzz about the seven-hour excursion. The rest of the group were going hiking in Glacier National Park. They'd be escorted by an off-duty park ranger, a friend of the McAllister family, who'd visited the Sundance the day before Jamie had arrived.

She'd heard all she wanted to hear about Seth's perfect ass, his bedroom blue eyes and the way he'd lifted Lily-from-San Francisco onto a horse as if she "hadn't weighed a thing."

God help her, Jamie honestly didn't think she could listen to any more of the silliness. She and her friends had often discussed men—admittedly ad nauseum at times—but these women were ridiculous. They never gave it a rest. Anyone would think they'd come halfway across the country just to get laid.

Sometimes they spoke openly in front of Rachel which made Jamie cringe all the way down to her toes. Three of the guys were her brothers, for heaven's sake. Although Rachel had been cagey about the website. She'd known what she was doing by posting the guys' pictures.

Still, it gave Jamie the willies to think Cole could consider her one of the pack. If that were the case, she didn't blame him for dodging her. That didn't mean she'd back off. Only that she had to be smarter and careful to prove to him she wasn't like the rest.

Besides, last night she'd been robbed. They'd almost kissed before being interrupted by that drunken lout Gunderson. There was no way in hell Jamie would ignore where that kiss could've led. Nor would she allow the incident to encourage Cole to keep his distance from her.

As soon as he parked the truck and climbed out, she moved away from the window and briefly listened to the laughter coming from the den. Good, everyone was busy reviewing tomorrow's activities. Now was the chance to catch him in private. But she didn't want him to think she'd been eagerly waiting for him.

She eyed the stairs, then ran up as fast as her tender thigh muscles would allow. If she timed it right, she'd be coming off the last step when he came through the door. Except when she got to the second floor and turned around, through the window she caught a glimpse of him disappearing into the stables.

"You did not just do that," she muttered, annoyed—with

him in general but more so with herself for acting like a twelve-year-old.

Jamie sighed and took baby steps down because sore muscles hadn't been enough punishment for her arrogance. Chafed skin and an aching butt had been added to the list of ouches, though the cream she'd bought at the variety store seemed to be helping. Not as much as Cole's liniment had, but at least she wasn't stinking up every room she entered.

She let herself out the front door, waved to a couple of older cowboys who left the bunkhouse and were headed toward a row of trucks. At any given time it looked like a used-car lot on the west side of the barn. She wondered how many employees worked at the Sundance and hoped that none of them were in the stables with Cole.

He was in the back when she entered. A dim light was on, and she heard the low murmur of his husky voice. She stopped to listen, not out of nosiness, but if he was talking to someone she didn't want to barge in on him. If he was talking to one of the horses…well, maybe she shouldn't barge in on that, either.

She stood, undecided, beginning to wonder if he'd feel ambushed by her.

His voice changed octaves and drifted out into the open.

"What can I do for you, Jamie?"

She jumped a little because she still couldn't see him, or figure out how he knew it was her. "If you're busy we can talk later."

"Come on back."

"I don't know where you are."

"The last stall on the right."

She continued toward the back, her eyes growing more accustomed to the dimness. The sun hadn't gone down completely but inside the shadowed stables it would be easy for someone unfamiliar with the hard, straw-strewn floor to misstep.

He was standing in front of a bay mare whose ears went back as soon as she spotted Jamie. "She's pregnant," he warned, "and irritable today, so better keep your distance."

Jamie nodded and glanced around. The stall was different from the rest—much larger, with a Plexiglas window on the side.

"That's a surveillance window," Cole said quietly, continuing to stroke the mare's neck. "So we can keep an eye on the old girl but not disturb her."

"This is a foaling box?"

Mild surprise lifted his brows. "Yep."

"I remembered from my uncle's peanut farm." She kept her gaze on the way the mare blew out short and hard through flared nostrils. "Maybe I shouldn't be here. I don't want to upset her."

"If Jezebel was upset, you'd know it. Isn't that right, girl?"

Jamie looked over and saw him smiling at the horse as he gently stroked her neck. He was different around animals, more relaxed, content. "What about you? Would you prefer I weren't here?"

He hesitated just enough to make her regret the question. "I don't mind."

"I got the feeling you might be avoiding me because of what happened with your neighbor last night."

He moved away from the mare, his lips pulled into a thin line. "I'm not avoiding anyone. Ranches don't run themselves."

Dammit, why had she brought up the incident? She honestly hadn't thought much about it. But of course Cole was still smarting. She would be, too, if someone had called her a whore, no matter what the context.

She blinked when she realized he was standing directly in front of her, waiting for her to move out of his way. He smelled surprisingly good for having been out in the heat all day, a pleasant citrus scent almost as if he'd recently taken a shower. But if he'd been home since she returned from town, she would've known.

A sudden thought struck her, a most unappealing thought... he could've been visiting a woman in town. Well, that idea totally sucked. Made sense though, since he hadn't made it home for dinner.

"So..." She stuck her hands in her back pockets as she slowly stepped backwards. "How was your meeting?"

"Too many opinions. Not enough problem-solving."

"Ah, so a normal run-of-the-mill meeting."

One side of his mouth lifted. "Pretty much. Look out."

"What?" She understood his warning when her butt made contact with a pole. "Oh." She automatically rubbed her bottom.

"Sore there, too?"

"Uh...that would make you grin because?"

He massaged the back of his neck, a pained expression on his face as he tried to pull back the smile. "Bad manners, I suppose."

Jamie laughed, made sure she cleared the pole and turned to walk with him past the stalls. "You missed dinner."

"I grabbed something at Marge's Diner."

"I met her today. She's quite a character."

Cole sort of grunted, and looked as though he was sorry he'd brought up the subject. "Can't believe a thing that woman says."

"About you?"

He flushed a little. "I expect she had something to say about everyone in town."

"Don't worry, I'm not one for gossip."

"Can't imagine that makes a bit of difference to Marge." He stopped to inspect a roan who'd stuck out its nose and whinnied.

"You're right about that." She sighed when she realized he wasn't going to take the bait and ask what she meant. It was supposed to be her opening to find out if he had a special woman in town.

His attention was solely on the horse as he worked his fingers up and down the animal's mane, frowning.

"What's wrong?" She tentatively reached out and touched the velvety nose.

"Ginger could use a good clipping and brushing."

"I can help with that. I think."

He sent her a faint smile. "Thanks, but it's not your job. The person who *is* responsible for her upkeep will be getting his backside in here tomorrow to do the job he was originally hired to do."

"Instead of catering to a herd of city fillies," she teased, using a man's deep voice.

He cocked a brow at her.

"I wasn't mimicking you. Just saying…"

"Good, because it would've been a lousy imitation."

Jamie grinned, thoroughly agreeing. He had a much huskier, sexier voice but she wisely kept the observation to herself. "Marge says you were against opening the ranch to guests."

"Oh, God."

"Want to know what else she had to say?"

"Not particularly."

"Really?"

For a second, he seemed torn, then shook his head. "Anything you hear around town is likely to be third- and fourth-hand information."

"The McAllisters have a sterling reputation. Everybody adores your family."

"Not everybody," he murmured, then clenched his jaw as if sorry he'd spoken his thoughts.

"Gunderson's an ass, and I don't want to talk about him, either, because he really screwed me up last night."

She saw the corners of Cole's mouth twitch with amusement. So what? It was true, he'd interrupted their kiss, dammit. "*Nobody* seems to like him." Cole abruptly turned his head, and she met his eyes with a chilly glare. "Don't look at me like that. I didn't say a word about last night. To anyone."

"Yeah, I appreciate that," he said slowly. "I filled Rachel in this morning."

"Why?" She pressed her lips together when she realized her response was inappropriate. "I just meant, why worry her… She's trying to make a go of the dude ranch, and none of the guests were involved."

"You're a guest."

That stopped her. "Well, yes, of course—" She was definitely an outsider, and how she could think otherwise even for a moment was beyond her. Slightly embarrassed, she cleared her throat, then tossed her head. "But since I'm staying on the same floor with the family I'm claiming squatters' rights."

Cole chuckled. "Ah. I'll be sure to pass that along."

"Don't you dare." She bumped him with her shoulder. It was a casual gesture, but she felt the electricity all the way down her arm. Good Lord, she hadn't been without sex that long, had she? "I do really like Rachel and your mom, and Hilda's great. She's like everyone's grandmother. She keeps us so well-fed I might have to go up a size."

He ran his gaze down her body, and not in a subtle way. "Mind grabbing that brush," he said, indicating a shelf of grooming supplies.

She walked over, conscious that he was probably checking out her ass. Fair enough. She'd already scoped his yesterday. "This one?"

"Yep." He turned back to Ginger's mane, a ghost of a smile tugging at his mouth.

"I thought you were going to leave the grooming for tomorrow."

"I want to get out a few of these tangles."

"God, I hope the horses won't be neglected because of the extra work."

"That's not going to happen." His jaw briefly tightened, but when the roan whickered, Cole relaxed and whispered something soothing, calming her.

Jamie liked watching him interact with the horse so she stood quietly as he ran the brush through Ginger's thick mane. She could see the tension leave his shoulders and it was really nice, so quiet but for a few whinnies. After a while she realized she should've offered to help. "Is there anything I can do?"

"I'm almost done, but don't wait around on my account."

She bristled at his remark. "You know, I really can be of some use if you let me."

"I'm sure you can, but for now you're on vacation. Go do fun things."

A flash of the women's conversation on the porch made her blink. Here she was, tingling and hot because of her proximity to this cowboy she'd only just met. Was she so different from the other guests, with their hunger so blatant and their desperation clinging to them like scented body spray?

She hoped so. She hadn't come to the ranch to get laid, though if Cole was interested she definitely wouldn't say no. If not, life would go on. "Hanging out with you tomorrow would be fun."

He stopped brushing and eyed her with skepticism as he returned the brush to the shelf. Without a word he picked up a bucket and started walking again.

She caught his arm where he'd rolled back his sleeve, and a muscle flexed beneath her palm. His flesh was warm with a sprinkling of dark hair and she wondered what his chest was like...smooth, a smattering of hair, she didn't have a preference, as long as he wasn't *too* hairy.

Her eyes were drawn to the unfastened top button of his blue Western-cut shirt. His skin was tanned and smooth, but she couldn't see enough, not nearly enough to give her a hint at his chest. She'd bet anything he wasn't overly muscled, just nicely defined. Her attention went back to his corded arm, and heat flared low in her belly.

Before she made a total fool of herself, she withdrew her hand. She doubted she'd get her way by ripping off his shirt. Some guys, yeah. But not Cole. "Why is that so hard to believe? I don't want to go white-water rafting tomorrow—I've done that before, a couple times. One of these days I would like to go hiking but I've also hiked in really cool places like the Himalayas and the Appalachian Trail. I've snorkeled in Hawaii and Fiji for a week, scuba-dived in Australia, piloted a houseboat down the Mississippi for a…well, frankly, too long…and *piloting* might be sugar-coating the experience, because I was really terrible at it." She shrugged, then noticed he'd narrowed his eyes as if he thought she was telling whoppers. "What?"

"You've really done all those things?"

She nodded. "It's kind of my job."

"Interesting." The frown was still there, causing his dark brows to dip. "Let me get rid of this bucket."

Disliking the defensiveness welling up inside her, she watched him stow the wooden bucket in a closet. She wasn't sure what caused the reaction, it wasn't as if he'd called her a liar, he just seemed surprised. Maybe it was the way he'd said "interesting" that bothered her.

"I write a travel blog," she said.

"Rachel mentioned something about that."

"I have quite a few followers, which means I get a lot of hits and sponsors, who pay for advertising. But it also means I have to shake things up, try new experiences, then write about them. Can't bore the readers."

"No, I suppose not." He turned for a final look at the two rows of stalls. "I don't imagine tagging along with me will give you anything exciting to write about."

"You'd be surprised."

His suspicious gaze shifted to her.

"I'm not talking about anything personal, for goodness sakes."

"I wasn't, either."

She stepped closer, aware that anyone walking by could see them. "I mean if you wanted to retry that kiss from last night…" She moistened her suddenly dry lips. "It wouldn't make the blog, or anything."

Cole coughed a little. "I would hope not."

"Are you referring to the kiss or writing about it?"

He swung a look toward the house and tugged at his shirt collar. She followed his gaze and realized anyone peering out the front window could see them, or at least him. She was far enough from the opening, but she had a mind to grab him by the shirt and pull him back inside.

She sighed. "I suppose if I'm totally bored or worried about material for the blog, I could head to town and hit up Marge. I'm sure she's a wealth of fascinating tidbits."

Snorting, he met her eyes. "You blackmailing me?"

"For a kiss? Nope." She smiled. "To get you to take me with you tomorrow? You bet."

His low husky chuckle danced along her nerve endings, tickled her insides. His eyes changed from milk chocolate to a rich, dark, irresistible temptation. "What's wrong with hanging out with the other ladies?"

"They make me crazy." She purposely whispered, forcing him to move closer in order to hear.

"What about Trace?"

"Trace who?"

His smile was slow, his gaze lazily lowering to her lips. "Those fancy trips you were talking about…you go with anyone?"

"Once upon a time I did, but things have changed and now it's only me." Judging from his expression, he'd misunderstood. Probably thought it was about a breakup and this was a rebound trip. "Occasionally either my cousin or one of my two best friends used to go with me. Now they're all married. The last fatality was a week ago."

She saw a flicker of pity in his face, and she looked away, gave a shrug of indifference. "Yep," she said, her mind scrambling to figure out what she'd said to elicit the reaction. "Linda could've been here with me, but she insisted on that trip to the altar instead. Her loss."

"What about your family? Where are they?"

"No brothers or sisters. My parents live in Switzerland. Job-related. Diplomatic service." She hoped he didn't ask anything more. Surrounded by a big loving family as he was, he'd never understand her relationship with her parents, and besides, she didn't like talking about them.

Somehow she always ended up in a position of trying to defend their choices. Defend her stilted relationship with them. She liked to think she'd made peace with not being put first and that she respected their sense of duty to their country. But if she let down her guard and thought too much…it rarely turned out well.

He studied her a moment, then moved closer and caught her chin. "I hate unfinished business," he murmured quietly as he lowered his mouth.

Her eyelids fluttered closed as his lips brushed hers. Somehow her breath got trapped in her chest. She felt behind her for the wall and pressed her palms against the rough unfinished wood. Shamelessly she let him do all the work, and he took his time, letting them get used to the contours of each other's mouth before using his tongue to trace her bottom lip, then entering.

Even though a part of her wanted to hurry him, she loved that he went slow, because slow meant thorough and she was pretty damn sure she'd never been kissed like this before. It was crazy because her response was anything but hesitant.

A fever raged inside that shocked her with its lightning-fast intensity.

She touched her tongue to his and Cole moved his hand from her chin to her throat. Her nipples tightened. He trailed a finger to the scoop of her neckline, and she completely forgot how to breathe. Placing his other hand on her waist, he deepened the kiss. She pushed off the wall and slid her arms around his neck. The move was purely reflexive, and too late she wondered where his fingers would have ended up.

His mouth slanted over hers, and she could feel the slight sting of stubble grazing her cheek. She didn't care. Not even a little. He tasted like heaven and sin wrapped up together, and her only regret was that they were still in the stable and not someplace private.

A second later, a phone rang. She ignored the sound, but then Cole drew back.

She blinked, dazed. "Is that me?" She patted her jeans' pocket. "Oh, you're kidding." She dug it out and fumbled trying to turn off the damn thing.

"Go ahead and get it."

"No way." She skimmed the lit screen. "Linda, you idiot, you're on your honeymoon," she muttered.

He stopped her from turning off the phone. "Might as well answer. Someone's coming."

"No." Her shoulders sagged and it struck her that she'd just whined like a two-year-old. Then she heard the murmur of approaching voices.

Cole smiled, brushed a brief kiss across her lips and moved back. "I'll see you later, okay?"

She brought the phone to her ear, stepped to the opening and morosely watched him stride off into the darkness. Night had fallen and she hadn't even known.

She gazed up at the cloud hiding the moon and pressed the button to receive the call. And then it dawned on her.

She shrieked into the phone. "Holy crap, Linda."

"What!"

"He said he'd see me later."

8

COLE TRIED TO sneak in through the kitchen, but Rachel was cutting up a carrot cake for the guests. He let her railroad him into stopping in the den for a few minutes where the women were discussing their upcoming activities.

Jamie was right. Most of them were on the overenthusiastic side, and he smiled thinking about how she'd be rolling her eyes at some of their untutored remarks. Trace ate it all up. He was more than happy to explain any misconceptions about running a ranch or white-water rafting, or any other topic, whether he knew spit about the subject or not.

What pleased Cole was how much his mother seemed to be enjoying the company. She smiled more, had a new spring to her step. He hadn't considered how lonely it was for her with only Hilda for company after Rachel had gone away to school. No denying the recent influx of cash from the dude ranch was welcomed, but the best payoff was seeing the light in his mom's eyes again.

He socialized for five minutes, ignored Rachel's evil eye when he excused himself, then took the stairs two at a time to get to his room. He wanted to grab a quick shower, get the dust out of his hair. More than likely the August heat had gotten to him and he was completely out of his mind. But he wasn't sorry he'd kissed Jamie, and he was hoping there'd be a knock at his door soon.

What would happen after that, he wasn't sure. After all his preaching to the hands to keep their heads on straight with the guests, he had a hell of a nerve. But Jamie was different. Even with that sharp city edge, she had a sweet wistfulness about her that drew him like a stallion to a mare in season.

Normally he was a fair judge of character, and he felt sure if anything happened between them she'd be discreet. He liked that she hadn't said anything about the Gunderson incident last night, and he'd bet Marge hadn't gotten a word out of Jamie that she hadn't wanted to part with.

Still, he'd hate if Rachel or his mother found out, even Trace. Jesse would be fine. He never got in Cole's business or expressed an unwanted opinion. He was the most cool-headed of the four of them, not that Cole would ever admit it to Jesse's face. No sense upsetting the apple cart.

He turned on the shower, and then peeled off his clothes while waiting for the water to heat. He caught a glimpse of his stubble-darkened jaw in the mirror, cursed himself and took out his razor. There was a chance he wouldn't see Jamie again tonight, or that all they'd do was talk, but…

Right. Only talk. Hell, he touched his semi-hard cock. One kiss and his body hadn't calmed down yet. Maybe he should do something about it now, instead of risking reacting like a frustrated sixteen-year-old.

Man, this wasn't like him. He never brought his personal business home. And after what that bastard Gunderson had said, anyone would think Cole would be watching his step, keeping his focus on pulling the Sundance out of the hole. But there was something compelling about Jamie, like an itch he'd eventually have to scratch. She'd only be here five more days. No sense wasting time once the sun was up.

JAMIE CAST A final glance in the dresser mirror, then grabbed the ointment Cole had left her last night. If she'd misunderstood him earlier, pretending to return the jar would ease some of her embarrassment.

Slowly she opened her bedroom door, hoping all doubt would be erased by him standing there ready to knock. No luck. Oh, God, she could be crazy wrong about his intention. That was the thing. If he'd seriously meant they'd see each other again tonight, he could've come to her. But he hadn't, and she was unwilling to let a paltry thing like—she swallowed—um, pride…stop her from being with Cole.

She did a quick hall check and then stepped over the threshold. No room for hesitation now, or she'd risk being spied by Rachel, or worse, Mrs. McAllister. So Jamie swiftly walked to his closed door, heard the downstairs grandfather clock chime ten and lifted her closed hand and knocked.

It was late. Cole normally woke before dawn. She was an idiot. Was she about to blow the rest of her week?

The door opened.

Cole stood there, his hand on the knob, his hair damp, his shirt hanging open. "Hey."

Dear God in heaven, yes, he had a damn fine chest. Smooth, surprisingly tanned, the perfect amount of definition.

She'd obviously stared too long.

"Oh, sorry." He'd glanced down, and was now hastily sliding buttons through holes.

She really wanted to stop him, tell him it was okay, more than okay, but she still had enough wits about her to keep her mouth shut and not make the situation worse.

"Come in," he said, and sadly, by now his shirt was mostly buttoned up. The man worked fast.

Not when he'd kissed her, though. He'd taken his time, his mouth slow and persuasive and…

Bad detour. She couldn't go there.

"I'd prefer you didn't stand in the hall like that," he said, moving farther back, presumably to give her space.

"Right." She slid a glance toward the staircase before slipping past him into his dimly lit room. "Sorry, I know it's late. I don't have to stay…. I just wanted to drop this off." She held up the jar, totally disgusted with herself for being a wuss. This wasn't like her.

He gave her a gentle smile that she should've drooled over, but that only made her feel more the idiot. "It's not late for me," he said, "but if you're uncomfortable being here we can talk tomorrow, or go to my study."

"Your study?" She shuddered, knowing it was located downstairs off the great room. "There are women down there."

"Quite a few of them," he agreed. "Here."

She glanced at the plain, straight-backed wooden chair he indicated, but she didn't sit. "Is this too weird for you?" She checked out the king-size bed with the hand-carved cherry headboard and matching dresser. "You know, with your mom and brothers and Rachel right down the hall?"

"I'm thirty-two. No one gets a say in what I do in my room. That said, I don't want to broadcast." His eyes gleamed with amusement. "We aren't doing anything that would cause brows to raise." He paused. "Are we?"

"Not yet."

Cole smiled. "You want a drink?"

Surprised, she glanced around.

"No, I don't generally drink alone, nor do I make it a habit of entertaining here. I grabbed a bottle from the kitchen."

"Oh, which would be…?"

"Whiskey. Best I could do."

"Then whiskey it is."

He walked over to the dresser and there was the bottle in plain sight, next to the lamp, which provided the only light. Of course she'd missed it, though. Her entire nervous system had been operating in high gear since their earlier encounter. While on the phone she'd run her mouth so fast that Linda had had to tell her to slow down. Jamie just hoped no one outside had overheard her schoolgirl babbling. She didn't think so. At least she'd had enough sense to walk toward the back of the stable for privacy.

Cole poured the amber liquid into two glasses. "I can run down and get ice if you want."

"No, this is fine." The truth was, she preferred beer or wine and didn't care for whiskey. But she was a bit more nervous than usual. No excuse, but there it was, so she'd give it a try.

She claimed the chair, then accepted the glass he offered, glad he'd given them each a judicious portion. Before he sat on the edge of his bed, she'd taken a small sip. But she made a face when the whiskey burned all the way down her throat.

"You want water with that?" he asked, concern wrinkling his brow.

"No, I'm good." She swallowed hard, trying to erase the strong taste. "What is this—Wild Turkey?"

"Nope, just plain ninety-proof firewater."

"Cooked up in your basement?"

He smiled, and drained his glass. "Guess I should've offered you one of those sissy drinks."

"Actually," she said with a sniff, "beer is my first choice."

"Mine, too, but only if it's cold."

"Depending on which hemisphere you find yourself, that isn't always possible." She thought for a second. "I once had some Ozark moonshine called Apple Pie that I found interesting."

"And? Did it taste like apple pie?"

"Not even close. More like Bananas Foster flambé. That sucker scorched my tonsils. I didn't think I'd be able to talk for a week."

Cole reached over and set his empty glass on the bedside table. "I might have downed a scorcher or two in my time. Now I like to see a label on the bottle before I tip it."

She smiled at the quaint way he put things. "Have you lived anywhere else but here?"

"I spent a year in Butte for school, but I didn't like that much."

"Butte or school?"

"Neither."

Jamie absently nodded, taking in the brown-and-taupe curtains, the patchwork comforter, and wondering if he'd had this same bedroom his whole life. She couldn't imagine staying in one place for any longer than four years. That was the extent of her tenure, first in college and then in her condo in West L.A., and then only because her friends were there.

"You're trying to figure out why I don't leave," he said, his matter-of-factness belied by an underlying defensiveness in his voice.

"Actually, I was trying to grasp what it would be like to stay in one place for so long."

His expression had changed to something bordering cynical. "Isn't that the same thing?"

"No," she said, surprised. "I understand why you'd want to stay—your family is here, the country is beautiful, you have deep roots here...." She took in a deep breath. "It's foreign to me, that's all. I think it's rather nice...." She let her voice trail off because the pity she'd seen earlier was in his eyes again, and she hated it, hated that she'd left herself unguarded. She pulled her shoulders back. "But you've traveled outside of Montana, right?"

"I've been to Wyoming and Idaho for rodeos and auctions or to pick up livestock. Not sure that counts." He shrugged, seemed relaxed again. "Can't say that I've been to a big city like New York or L.A."

"Sometimes it's fun to have plays and concerts and a variety of restaurants at your disposal, but a larger city certainly has its drawbacks."

"But you live in L.A."

"True..." She almost added that she'd bought her condo because her friends were there, except that had changed and she did not want to stir that pot again. She polished off the small sip of whiskey, tried not to shudder and set her glass beside his. "Tell me more about you."

"You've pretty much heard everything," he said with a dry laugh. "This ranch has been, and I expect always will be, my life."

"I can see that. You belong here."

He studied her for a moment, as if mulling over what and how much he wanted to say. "I decided to join the army at one point. I was nineteen and figured I owed Uncle Sam a few years. A recruiter explained to my friend Noah and I that if we enlisted on the buddy system we'd do our tours together. Didn't work out."

"They lied?"

"No." He seemed amused by her leap to judgment. "It was real enough, though I don't think they do it anymore. This was thirteen years ago." He hesitated, and when she stared expectantly at him, he said, "Hell, might as well spit it out. Noah reminds me often enough."

"Noah? He's the sheriff?"

"Yep, Noah Calder. Known him since… Well, I guess we've always known each other." He got up, poured himself another shot of whiskey. This time half as much as the first.

"I didn't mean to sidetrack you." She leaned forward. By the why-did-I-bring-this-up look on Cole's face, she could tell this was going to be good. "Go on."

He took an unhurried sip. "I'm assuming you don't want a refill."

She snorted. "Don't try and change the subject."

The corners of his mouth lifted in a smirk and he sat down again, stretching out his long legs in front of him. He had on socks, no boots, and their feet were only inches apart. A totally juvenile thing to get mushy over, but she shivered anyway. Briefly considered that if he wanted to kiss her instead, she'd let him off the hook.

"It's not a big deal. Noah and I signed on the dotted line. Then when it was time to show up, turns out I was allergic to the wool in the uniform and they said thanks but no thanks."

She gaped at him. "So Noah got his hair buzzed off and you got to come home."

"Pretty much."

"Oh, nice." She tried not to laugh and failed.

"Hey, as soon as he was out he got GI Bill money to finish school, so no crying a river for him."

"But he hasn't let you live it down."

He shook his head, a deadpan expression on his face. "We'll both be ninety, rocking on that porch outside and he'll still be telling the damn story."

"Well, it's funny, but then it's not." Jamie sighed. "Sheesh, it's like all my friends getting married en masse and leaving me in the dust." She realized how that sounded and shifted her gaze away from him.

"Even Noah would agree it worked out the way it was supposed to. My father passed away a year later," Cole said quietly. "Jesse was already off at school. Trace and Rachel were still young. Mom couldn't have handled the ranch by herself."

"I'm so sorry. I didn't know."

He shrugged. "It was cancer. We had some warning. Not enough." He finished the glass of whiskey. "But then I guess it's never enough."

She leaned over and touched his leg, wanting to give comfort, nothing else. He closed a hand over hers, squeezing gently, then returned his glass to the nightstand.

"Your mom was still young."

"Only forty-three."

"It's been eleven years." Jamie hoped she wasn't overstepping. "Widowed that young, did she ever consider remarrying?"

"I don't think so. She never seemed interested in anyone. 'Course Fred Hutchins and Roger Limb were the only two men brave enough to risk getting past me and my brothers, and they were never candidates."

"Seriously? Did you run anyone off?"

"Damn right I did. I kept a shotgun next to the front door."

"Cole!"

"Don't worry. No shots were fired. No threats made. The shotgun never left the closet. In the beginning there might have been a few narrowed-eyed warnings, but that's it," he added with a shrug.

She suppressed a grin. "I guess that was only natural. You guys were still young."

"Rachel said it didn't matter what anyone said or did. Dad was the love of Mom's life. She would never have settled for anyone else."

"Wow. You think that's true?" She sounded so sentimental and wistful that it embarrassed her. "I mean, that's nice. Sweet, but sad, too, you know? So many divorces these days, or worse, couples living with indifference."

He looked confused. "I got the impression your parents are still together."

"They are, and actually they're a very good match. They both consider duty to their country their number-one priority." She saw the curiosity in his eyes, and quickly added, "I admire their loyalty and commitment."

"I understand," he said, then sighed. "Despite what Noah might tell you, I had every intention of fulfilling my military obligation."

"Hmm, I'd like to meet this Noah."

"Is that right?" He shocked her by leaning over and grabbing her hand. With a gentle tug he had her on her feet.

Jamie voluntarily took the couple steps necessary to wedge herself between his spread legs. She touched his strong angular jaw. His skin was warm and smooth. He'd taken the time to shave, and he smelled of soap and water and heat. She filled her lungs with his heady masculine scent and whispered, "I wish you'd left your shirt unbuttoned."

"That would've been rude," he said, a small smile threatening the corners of his mouth. His head was tipped back, not much though, because he was so tall that even with him sitting his head came up past her shoulders.

"And probably foolish."

"That, too."

"Or not." She moved her hand to toy with his top button, and all she could think about was pulling that shirt off him. Being able to feel his naked chest against her tight aching nipples. She moistened her dry lips, and his gaze lowered to her mouth.

"Damn, I want you," he murmured, resting his hands on her hips.

"I don't see the problem."

"I swore to myself—" He exhaled a harsh breath that felt hot and fiery against her collarbone. "Christ, Jamie..."

Their lips met in a heated rush, and his arms came around her, his hands cupping her bottom until she arched against him. She pushed a hand through his damp hair, and though he started slow, his mouth grew more demanding, until he'd pushed his tongue between her lips and swept inside.

Her unsteady fingers slid to his chest so she could continue to free his buttons until she'd managed to unfasten them all without ripping anything. The way his arms were bent, she couldn't successfully push off his shirt, but she slid her hands inside and stroked his bare muscled back.

Cole let go of her, and she whimpered a protest before guessing his intent. He shrugged off his shirt, then grabbed the hem of her stretchy top and yanked it over her head. He tossed it over his shoulder; the whole time his gaze was raking her face and the front of her pink lacy bra. He found the clasp between her breasts and opened it with a single flick.

Her taut nipples were flushed and beaded, and he circled

one with the rough pad of his thumb. She quivered inside, or maybe her entire body reacted, she wasn't sure, all of her senses were on full alert.

He cupped the weight of her breast, and when it seemed touch wasn't enough, he rolled his tongue over the nipple, tasting and nibbling, then tugging the tight bud into his mouth. She shivered almost uncontrollably, and he froze, lifted his head, searched her face.

"Don't stop," she whispered. "Please don't."

Moaning deep in his throat, he wrapped both arms around her, lifted her onto the bed and laid her back. She rubbed her palm across his straining fly, and he sucked in a sharp breath. Her shoulder came off the bed as she reached for him, anxious to unzip his jeans, but the force of his mouth pressed her back against the mattress. He tasted her lips, then licked at the hollow of her throat and trailed a warm moist path to her other breast.

He found her nipple and traced it with the stiff point of his tongue before sucking her into his mouth. His hand trembled with what she presumed was an attempt at restraint as he gently kneaded her other breast. Knowing that he was having trouble controlling himself released a surge of fiery warmth that rushed through her veins as she grabbed hold of his bulging biceps.

As he used his hands, his teeth and his tongue on her mouth and breasts, she slipped her other hand between them, splaying her fingers across his chest, loving the feel of his taut warm skin against her palm. Loving that his nipples were nearly as responsive as her own.

"You're perfect, Jamie. Beautiful and perfect," he murmured against her breasts, and the vibration of his lips sent a shaft of pure pleasure through her.

Or maybe it was the words themselves that had her floating a foot off the mattress. No one had ever said anything like that to her before, and had it been any other man she wouldn't have believed for a second that he meant it. Easier to imagine the sentiment as a meaningless attempt at foreplay. But Cole wasn't that kind of guy.

He kissed the valley between her breasts, then kissed the sensitive skin leading to her navel. With one hand he unsnapped her jeans and slowly drew down the zipper.

She closed her eyes, not lifting a finger to help him. Her turn to undress him was coming, but if he didn't hurry she wouldn't be able to wait.

His hand abruptly stilled.

She opened her eyes in time to see a flash of light behind the drawn curtains. No, it wasn't a flash after all. Someone had turned on the outside floodlights.

Then came the yelling.

9

COLE MET HER EYES, then allowed himself a final glimpse of her smooth flushed skin. Battling every primitive instinct he possessed, he pulled away from Jamie and walked to the window. He shoved aside the curtain and saw Dutchy and Josh hurrying from the barn toward the house, grim looks on their faces.

Half expecting to see Gunderson being escorted off the property, Cole surveyed the area and saw several of the other hands in various stages of undress milling around outside the bunkhouse and barn. Kyle and Chester were crouched down by the driveway, inspecting something in the dirt.

"What's going on?"

He turned and saw that Jamie had gotten to her feet. She still wore jeans, but no top, her firm high breasts still bare.

His cock twitched. He wasn't as hard as he was a minute ago, but staring at her didn't help.

"I don't know." He found his shirt on the floor. "I've got to go find out."

"Can I go with you?" She quickly searched the bed, then the floor and scooped up her bra.

"Probably not a good idea," he said, shrugging on his shirt.

"Oh, right."

He knew Dutchy and Josh would've reached the front door by now but he heard nothing. For an old house, the place was well insulated and soundproof, though he suspected Trace had answered their knock.

She picked up his boots from where he'd left them in the corner and brought them to him. He repaid her thoughtfulness by trying not to stare at her breasts. It was damn hard. While he sat at the edge of the bed and pulled on his boots, she helped him out by slipping on the lacy bra.

"Whatever's happening," he said, "lousy timing." He caught her hand as he stood, and pulled her close.

She slid her arms around his waist and looked up at him, her eyes dark instead of the usual warm golden-green. "Be safe."

"I'm sure it's nothing." He brushed back the hair from her face and lightly kissed her lips. It was a mistake. He wanted so much more than a brief kiss but he had to go. "If you wait a few minutes, Rachel will be out there and you can come see for yourself."

"Okay, I will."

Mistake number two. He shouldn't have encouraged her to come outside. Really stupid move. He was a mess inside. His body still hadn't calmed down, and as much as he wanted her, he equally wanted to kick himself for not having had more willpower. He wasn't a kid. Acting on impulse wasn't his style, so what the hell? Jesus, she was a guest at the ranch and he'd just met the woman. Sex wasn't the problem. It was the weird connection he felt with her that made no sense. Made him a little nervous.

By the time he walked through the front door, a whole crowd had gathered outside: Rachel, Trace, a few of the guests and most of the hands. They all looked at him as if he'd finally found his misplaced invitation to the party.

"What's going on?" He directed the question at Dutchy,

their foreman, but he and Trace both started talking at once. "Hold on, one of you at a time."

"It's the Exiss," Dutchy said, yanking the battered black Stetson off his balding head and shooting a reluctant glance at Josh.

"What about it?" Cole asked.

"It's missing."

Cole hoped like hell he'd heard wrong. The horse trailer was their newest purchase. "It's what?"

Josh stuffed his hands in his jeans pockets and visibly swallowed. "I know it's my fault. I shoulda put it with the others, but I was late for supper and I left it in back of the barn."

"Wait a minute." Cole shook his head. "A horse trailer doesn't just hook itself up and drive away. You sure it's not parked in the lean-to?"

Josh stared at the ground, kicking at the dirt with the toe of his scuffed boot. "I'm sorry, boss. I truly am, but I'm real clear on having left it behind the barn."

"It's gotta be Gunderson," Trace said, his shoulders tense and his jaw clenched. "That bastard needs a good asskicking."

"Don't jump to conclusions," Cole warned, even though Trace had echoed Cole's thoughts exactly. "How did you know it was missing? You had to have heard something."

Josh shook his head. "I came out for a smoke before bed and was walking around, looking at the moon when it struck me there was a big ol' empty space where the trailer shoulda been." He scrubbed at his long narrow face. "Earlier I heard a truck, but it sounded like Kyle's. Dammit, I'm sorry, boss. Wouldn't blame you if you fired me right here on the spot."

"Let's worry about locating the trailer." Cole tried to keep his cool. Fitted-out horse trailers were damn expensive. They couldn't afford to buy another one. He heard murmuring and looked over at two of the guests whispering to each other. He'd almost forgotten they were there. "Rachel." He motioned with his eyes for her to step aside with him. "Everyone doesn't need to be out here," he said in a quiet voice.

"You're right." Her sympathetic gaze went to Josh, and she gave him a small reassuring smile before herding the guests back inside.

"All right." Cole faced the men. "I want everyone to think about the last couple of hours since it got dark. You remember hearing anything unusual that you didn't think much of at the time?"

He got a few blank looks, a lot of head-shaking, and then Dutchy said, "I was playin' poker with the boys till nine. My luck got to runnin' kind of muddy so I hit the sack." He shrugged his bony shoulders. "My bunk's on the barn side but I didn't a hear a thing till Josh came barrelin' in all excited."

"We're wasting time," Trace said, his temper plainly coursing hot. "I say we ride over to Gunderson's place."

"And do what? Accuse a man without any proof?" Cole gave him a stern look. He didn't want to dress his brother down in front of the men but he wouldn't hesitate to pull him inside for it.

"I'm not suggesting we accuse him, just poke around his property."

"That's trespassing."

"He has no problem waltzing onto McAllister land." Trace was obviously spoiling for a fight, and man, Cole did not need that right now.

"I'd call Noah before I cross onto another man's property uninvited," he said. "You know better, Trace. Let's keep a cool head."

"Are you gonna call the sheriff?" Dutchy asked. "'Cause you know I dislike Gunderson as much as any man here, but truth be told, this ain't the first theft this week."

Frowns were exchanged, heads scratched and silence stretched for an eternity.

"Good point, Dutchy." Cole almost hated to admit it. "We have to consider that maybe Mrs. Clements was a victim, too."

"Did the sheriff believe her?" Josh asked. "Everyone I know thought she misplaced the four-wheeler."

"What difference does it make?" Trace said irritably. "That won't get back our trailer."

"I know that." Josh hung his head. "I'll pack up my things now if you want."

"No," Trace and Cole said at the same time.

"Anybody else happen to be outside since nightfall?" Cole was pretty steamed but he wouldn't fire the kid. He was only twenty-one and a good worker, even if he had left out the trailer. The fact was, during the summer they often left out the older trailers and everyone made mistakes.

Cole was no exception, he thought glumly as he caught a glimpse of Jamie standing near the porch. His stomach cramped in a sickening rush of guilt. Here he was asking if anyone had been around, and where had he been?

Logically he knew it didn't matter that he'd been kissing Jamie, stripping her naked, on the verge of making love to her. If she hadn't been here, chances were he'd have been in his room anyway, probably asleep and unaware of an intruder. But he apparently was in a mood to let his thinking be clouded because the tension in his belly wouldn't ease.

He purposely positioned himself so that he couldn't see her and hoped like hell she'd go back into the house. "Chester, I saw you and Kyle crouched by the driveway. You find tracks?"

"A whole mess of 'em." Chester spread his hands. "Nothing that would help."

Cole nodded. "I don't see any point in dragging Noah out here this time of night. He won't find anything we haven't. I'll call him in the morning. You guys try and get some sleep."

"Shit, Cole, I still say—"

"Trace, no one is going to Gunderson's." He met his brother's defiant glare, and gave him a stern look in return. "Get a flashlight and meet me by the barn."

"I wish Jesse were home. He's not so hardheaded," Trace muttered as he turned toward the house.

"Where is Jesse?" Dutchy asked. "Still in Wyoming?"

Cole nodded. "He'll be back in the morning." Under the guise of tracking Trace, he swung a look toward the porch. Jamie was gone. "No need to stay up. I don't expect we'll find anything, but it might help Trace let off some steam."

"I figured as much." Dutchy plopped his hat on his head. "If it's all the same to you, I'll have a look around with you two boys."

"Suit yourself." Cole glanced up at the second story.

Jamie was standing at the window. She was in her own room. Good. She was going to have to stay there. Enough mistakes had been made tonight.

JAMIE HADN'T EXPECTED Cole to knock on her door last night. She knew something had been stolen, and she'd seen the concern on his face. Nevertheless she had hoped to catch him before he left this morning. But by the time she'd run downstairs at six, he was gone.

"Pass me the lime marmalade, would you?"

She had the horrible feeling that he was trying to avoid her. Naturally she understood why he'd been tied up last night, but...

Brenda elbowed her. "Jamie?"

"What?"

"The lime marmalade?"

She blinked. "Oh, sorry." She reached for the glass bowl brimming with Hilda's special recipe. It was a huge breakfast hit with all of the guests, and she was surprised there was that much left. Though the bowl could've been refilled three times and she wouldn't have noticed.

"You look tired," said the blonde sitting across from Jamie, and darn if she could remember the woman's name. She bore too much of a resemblance to her friend, both bottle-blondes with spray-on tans and frighteningly white teeth. "Even with all the excitement last night, I crashed hard. Must be the mountain air." She glanced coyly at her roommate. "Adele couldn't sleep. She was too busy sitting at the window watching Cole."

Adele rolled her eyes and sipped her coffee.

The other four women at the table grinned.

Jamie silently cleared her throat. She didn't blame the woman for ogling Cole. He was hot. And he was hers. At least for the next five days. "Does anyone know if they found whatever it was they were looking for?" she asked casually, and buttered her biscuit.

"Who knows? I just hope that cute sheriff comes by before we go white-water rafting." The chatty blonde wrinkled her nose. "Rachel said stuff like this never happens around here, but it was kind of exciting. Do you think it was all staged for our benefit?"

"Seriously?" Jamie hadn't realized she'd spoken aloud until everyone stared at her. Not in a good way, either.

Thankfully, Rachel's entrance into the dining room distracted everyone. Jamie met her eyes, saw the smile she was holding back and knew she'd overheard.

"How's the coffee? Need a refill?" Rachel lifted the silver carafe. "More biscuits or fruit?"

Everyone shook their heads, and then questions were asked about their day's activities.

Jamie poured more desperately needed caffeine down her throat while she watched Rachel interact with the other women. She was a puzzle, that was for sure. Rachel seemed smart, had a masters degree in hotel management, and she'd obviously known what she was doing when she created the ranch's website. She was terrific at marketing and a wonderful hostess. What Jamie couldn't figure out was how she could be content living here where her opportunities were limited.

Granted it was her home and all her family was right here, but she'd been away at school for over six years and had seen there was more to the world than her little corner of Montana. As far as Jamie could tell, there weren't many men around who someone like Rachel would be interested in dating—not to mention she'd probably known all the guys close to her age since kindergarten.

Some of the hired hands were nice and most of them were fairly good-looking, a dream for a single woman who was visiting for a week, but not for Rachel. Jamie couldn't see her with any of them. Did she feel trapped now that she was growing the dude ranch side of the business? Was she biding her time, making her contribution before she planned her escape?

God, Jamie had no idea why she was contemplating any of this nonsense. Not only was none of it her business, but she didn't really know Rachel. She was simply projecting. For all she knew, Rachel might want to be married with four kids, stay at home and churn butter.

Nah, Jamie was never that far off on her first impressions. She brought the cup to her lips and made a face. The coffee was barely lukewarm.

"I figured it was cold by now."

She looked up and saw Rachel with her hands full of plates and leftover bowls of fruit. Everyone else had left the table and they were exiting the dining room.

"Um." Jamie blinked. "Guess I spaced out a minute."

"I saw that dazed look." Rachel grinned. "Come on, we have fresh coffee in the kitchen."

Jamie got up, grabbed the basket of biscuits and, balancing three dirty cups, followed Rachel.

"I didn't mean to put you to work," Rachel said when she turned and saw Jamie set her load on the counter by the sink.

"What, you think I'd sashay in here with free hands?"

"You *are* a guest."

"Oh, please." Jamie eyed the huge coffee station. "I won't turn down that cup you promised."

"Of course…" Rachel set down the fruit and wiped her hands with a dish towel.

Jamie waved her off. "I'll get it."

"Keep this up and we'll have to refund your money."

"Ah, rules number one and two, never hesitate to grab a deposit, and strike the word *refund* from your vocabulary."

Rachel laughed. "So you're more than a pretty face and gadabout travel blogger."

Jamie smiled wryly. "Let's say I learned the hard way during the initial stages of my blog."

"Yes, I'm beginning to see I have a lot to learn, too. Getting this place started has been pretty overwhelming." Rachel glanced over her shoulder toward the kitchen door that led to the mudroom and then outside. "I had to chase Hilda and my mother out this morning. They've been burning the candle at both ends."

"As I'm sure you're doing, especially handling the website and reservations."

"Yeah, but they have thirty years on me. I don't want to work them to death. And now, with the added stress of last night…" She opened the dishwasher and sighed. "And God only knows why I'm telling you all of this."

Jamie shrugged. "It's nice to be included." That sounded wrong, not at all what she meant. "I'm glad you feel comfortable with me."

Rachel transferred a stack of plates from the counter to the sink, then gave Jamie a long thoughtful look. "I do. I'm not sure why, except that you remind me of one of my sorority sisters. I bet if you lived here we'd be friends."

"I bet we would, too." Jamie took a sip of the hot coffee then seized the opening Rachel had handed her. "Do you plan on staying here in Montana?"

The surprise in the other woman's eyes turned guarded. "I love it here. I can't imagine…" She shook her head. It seemed clear to Jamie that this was a sore subject and not open for discussion. "Living away at school was fun. I had a blast, but there's no place for me like Montana."

"It is beautiful." Jamie set down her cup and went to the sink to rinse the dishes. The window above framed part of the Rockies and she stared out at the breathtaking view. "I can understand you wanting to stay." She passed Rachel a plate. "You have a special guy hidden away?"

"Wouldn't that be cool?" Rachel sighed and continued to load the dishwasher. "The downside of living in a small town."

"No proverbial high-school sweetheart?"

Rachel's short laugh sounded bitter. "Right. Matt Gunderson. I was still a senior when he left town."

"Gunderson?" Jamie nearly choked.

"I know, right?" Rachel smiled. "You should see your face."

The slam of a car door saved her from responding. They both looked out the window, craning their necks to see who'd pulled up out front.

Jamie had a better view. "I think it's the sheriff."

"Yup, that's Noah." Rachel dried her hands. "Cole called him. Let's go see what's going on."

"Um, I don't think I should."

"Why not?" Rachel pulled out a dry dish towel and pushed it on Jamie.

"Because it's none of my business?"

"Do you want to know?"

"Hell, yeah."

Rachel chuckled. "Then come on. I just made you an honorary member of the family."

Jamie quickly dried off and hurried after Rachel through the dining room and into the foyer. As soon as she saw Cole from the front window, Jamie's heart started to pound. She hoped he didn't have a problem with her tagging along with Rachel. If he did, oh well… Nothing to do about it.

Noah was walking toward Cole, who'd just ridden in from somewhere past the barn and was handing over the reins of his horse to one of the wranglers.

"What about Noah?" Jamie whispered while they were still on the porch. "You ever go out with him?"

"God, no. He's like one of my brothers." Rachel gave her an amused glance. "Why, are you interested?"

"No," she said, a little too vehemently. He was totally hot, but her eyes were on Cole and just the sight of him made her melt a little.

"Didn't think so," Rachel murmured in a smug voice.

"What's that supposed to mean?"

"I don't think you want me answering now," she said in a hushed tone as they came up on Cole and Noah.

Jamie exhaled in a whoosh. Crap. Was she that obvious with Cole?

Both men looked over at them and lapsed into silence. They hadn't had time to get into a serious discussion yet so Jamie didn't feel too bad about interrupting.

"Mornin', Rachel," Noah said, his gaze sliding to Jamie. He smiled, touched the brim of his hat. Light brown hair, blue-green eyes. Very hot. Bummer for Rachel that he was more like a brother.

"This is my friend, Jamie," Rachel said, by way of introduction, then slipped into business mode. "You know anything yet?"

Startled, Jamie blocked out Noah's answer, barely registering the flicker of surprise on Cole's face. Rachel had referred to her as a friend, not as one of the guests, or just plain Jamie. Warmth blossomed in her chest and crawled up her neck.

Nothing unpleasant, it was just that Rachel's casual inclusion was so unexpected…so touching.…

Good Lord, her reaction was crazy. Jamie had friends, for goodness sake. Really good friends. The best. She wasn't that scared twelve-year-old kid anymore, standing on the outside looking in, not quite getting the private jokes or looks. She was feeling a bit adrift, but that didn't mean anything in the long run. She'd built herself an independent life, one that she was damn proud of. This was a brief fling, that was all. With Cole, with Rachel, with the illusion of a family. It felt great, but it was temporary. Exactly the way she liked things.

10

"I'VE GOT ROY AND GUS going door-to-door," Noah said. "So far no one saw anything unusual last night or this morning. We've been warning folks to check their fields and barns to make sure they don't have equipment missing, too."

Cole would be surprised if the deputies turned up anything and he knew Noah well enough to believe he felt the same way. "We had a few transients looking to hire on last month." Cole picked up his hat, ran a hand through his hair, and then resettled the Stetson on his head. "They were headed north but there's no more work up there than down here. It's possible they came back through and were desperate enough to take whatever they thought would bring in a few bucks."

Without being rude, or giving Jamie the impression that he was avoiding her, he kept his body angled toward Noah. Why Rachel had felt compelled to bring Jamie out here with her was beyond him. Jamie distracted him, and that was the last thing he needed right now. Look where cozying up to her had gotten him last night.

Obviously keeping his eyes averted from her wasn't enough to stay focused. Noah had said something, and Cole had no idea what it was. So they just kept staring at each other until Cole chanced a small shrug and hoped it was answer enough.

Noah hooked his thumbs in the front pockets of his jeans. He'd worn his gun today, which was unusual. "I know you think Gunderson had something to do with it. Wouldn't surprise me if he did, but I've got no evidence to warrant searching his property."

"When Wallace is sober, he's not stupid," Rachel said. "If he arranged to steal that trailer, it's long gone."

"You make a good point." Noah paused for a moment. "Gunderson wouldn't have done the deed himself. He'd have arranged it with one of his men. Friday's payday." A sly smile tugged at Noah's mouth. "You could get your boys to hit Sadie's bar. A couple of those young bucks from Colorado that Wallace hired last year can't hold their liquor worth spit. If they know anything at all, well—"

"I always did like you, Noah." Rachel turned her grin on Jamie. "You and I should go to Sadie's on Friday. I bet we could loosen those boys' lips."

"Jesus, Rachel." Cole sighed with disgust. "Don't go dragging your guests into this," he said, and caught the glint of temper in Jamie's eyes. He couldn't identify the cause, but it was directed at him.

"Hey, I'm in." Jamie lifted a hand, and Rachel high-fived her. Then Jamie gave him a satisfied smirk. "Don't you worry about your *sister's guest*. I have a mind of my own, thank you."

The emphasis she'd put on "sister's guest" told him all he needed to know. Hell, how had she expected him to refer to her? "No," he said, setting his jaw when the two women glared at him as if he'd suggested they run him a hot bath and serve him supper in bed. "The answer's no."

"Huh. I don't recall the question." Jamie's brows rose, her gaze pointedly locking on him for a few seconds before turning to Rachel. "Do you?"

"Nope." His sister was doing a piss-poor job of keeping a straight face. Never could. That's why the boys liked playing poker with her. "Did you bring a sundress or anything sexy to wear?" she asked Jamie. "If not I bet I have something that'll fit you."

"I only packed one dress, but I think it'll work. Let's go see." Ignoring him and Noah, talking and laughing, the women headed for the house.

Cole stared after them. "Goddammit."

"Sorry, buddy, didn't mean to cause trouble," Noah said, the amusement in his voice fueling Cole's foul mood. "Should've known better than to make that suggestion in front of Rachel. Here I was worried about saying too much in front of the blonde."

"Her name's Jamie," Cole said irritably.

"Ah, that's right." Noah knew her name. He was just trying to get a rise out of Cole. Which he had.

"I don't need shit from you." Cole massaged the kink in his neck.

Noah laughed. "No use telling Rachel to give up the idea. Once she gets it in her head to do something, it's hard to pry the notion loose."

"I'll talk to her, anyway."

"You might have better luck talking to Jamie." Noah paused. "What's going on there?"

"Jamie?" Cole shrugged. "She's only been here a couple of days." He stared toward the house, even though the women had disappeared inside.

"Making the sparks flying between you two all the more surprising."

"Sparks?" Cole frowned. Man, he hoped Noah was imagining things. Had to be Jamie getting her nose out of joint over him calling her Rachel's guest. All the more reason to keep his distance. The last thing he needed was for anyone to find out about what he and Jamie had been doing last night.

"It's not like that," Cole murmured. "She won't be here that long."

Noah's cell rang and he answered the call.

Cole half listened, knowing that it was Wade, one of the deputies, on the other end. While Noah was distracted, Cole mulled over how he was going to get Rachel to drop the foolishness over going to Sadie's. The idea was still worthwhile. He'd have to make her see that Josh and Kyle going to the bar to shoot pool and drink beer on payday wasn't out of the ordinary. Her suddenly showing up would be.

He caught part of Noah's conversation. Sounded as if something had happened at the T&J. He listened more closely until Noah hung up.

Exhaling sharply, Noah slid his cell phone into his breast pocket. "The moon is full and the crazies are out."

"Another theft?"

"Harlan Roker says he's missing a trailer."

"A horse trailer?"

"Nah, a small flatbed. Didn't know it was gone till Roy started asking questions, but now Harlan is all fired up, especially with his sons away at the Billings rodeo. Of course Avery is right there alongside him kicking dirt. You know he's gonna try to convince everyone that you McAllisters are to blame for bringing in outsiders."

"Spread the word that before they leave all guests' luggage will be checked for stolen four-wheelers and trailers."

Noah smiled and glanced over his shoulder toward the barn. "I'm headed over to Harlan's now, see if I can calm down the old man." He scanned the stables. "You might think about posting night watch until we get a handle on what's going on."

"I already spoke to Dutchy about it." Cole walked him to his truck. "I'm taking the first watch myself tonight."

The front door to the house opened, and the sound of feminine laughter spilled out into the bright sunny morning. Trace led his group of enthusiastic white-water rafters onto the porch. Daisy Duke shorts and skimpy halter tops seemed to be the uniform of the day.

"I'm outta here." Noah quickly climbed into his truck, then from the safety of his cab, he put up his hand in a brief no-nonsense wave.

"Chickenshit," Cole muttered before he closed the driver's-side door.

Noah just smiled, started the engine and reversed the truck.

Trace jogged over to Cole. "Anything?"

He shook his head. "Harlan Roker says he's missing a trailer. Noah's on his way over there now."

"This makes no sense. None of this. What the hell's going on, Cole?" Trace frowned after the sheriff's vehicle.

"I don't know, but starting tonight we're going to keep a man outside from sundown to sunup. We'll split each watch in two. I'll go first."

"I don't mind following on your heels."

Cole glanced toward the women starting to look impatient while they waited for Trace by his truck. He had a feeling his brother was gonna be tired tonight. "I'll see how Dutchy worked it out. Go take care of your field trip."

"I dunno…" Trace said, concern clouding his boyish face. "I should get one of the other guys to take them."

Cole clapped his shoulder. "Nothing more you can do here, little brother. Nothing either of us can do. Stick to the plan, and keep this low-key. I don't want to advertise that we'll be posting watch. If anybody asks about last night, just tell them the sheriff is looking into the theft."

Trace nodded. "Jesse called. Something came up on his rescue. He'll be back late this afternoon."

"You fill him in?"

"Ma talked to him, not me."

"Okay. Go. Your harem is waiting." Cole smiled at Trace's snort of disgust.

"This dude ranch business was fun the first week. Not so

much anymore," he grumbled in a low voice before plastering on his lady-killer grin and striding toward his adoring fans.

Cole watched him, wondering how many guest rooms the kid had snuck into since the ranch opened. Trace wasn't a bastard about it, but he'd always been popular with the ladies. Hell, he'd been proposed to twice his senior year in high school. As soon as Rachel had proven serious about booking guests, Cole had pretty much known he'd lose Trace.

Not that Cole was complaining. Didn't have the right even if he were so inclined. He wasn't getting much done himself. Although his problem was a bit more narrow in scope. In fact, his problem had just walked out onto the porch.

No way he could pretend he hadn't seen Jamie. If he thought he could've gotten away with heading for the north pasture he would've swung into his saddle and ridden as fast as humanly possible. When he was around that woman he didn't have the sense God gave a gnat.

He eyed Tango, who was busy munching on hay, and resignedly waited for her.

She stopped in front of him and placed her hands on her hips. "You're avoiding me."

"I had business with the sheriff."

"I know that, but you could barely look at me."

"What do you want, Jamie?"

"It's what I don't want," she said. "I don't want you to regret what happened between us last night."

"Nothing happened. I think I would've remembered." The hurt in her eyes made him wish he'd chosen his words more carefully.

"That surprises me. I admit it." She visibly swallowed. "I wouldn't have guessed you to be so dismissive after what we…" Her shoulders sagged. "You know what? Forget it. You win."

"Hey, wait." He caught her arm, preventing her from walking away. It was probably a mistake. If he'd let her go, maybe she'd be the one doing the avoiding and he could stop thinking about her. "Trust me, I'm not dismissing last night."

"What is it, then?"

"Not once, for as far back as I can remember, have we ever had anything stolen off this ranch. Not so much as a gallon of fuel."

"That's quite remarkable with such a large operation," she said slowly, confusion creasing her brow. "But I don't see how that has anything to do with you and me."

They were standing out in the open, and he was still holding her arm. He let her go and rubbed his palms down the front of his jeans. "I'm responsible for this place."

"Yes, I understand." Her gaze sharpened and locked steadily on his. "But you weren't responsible for the theft last night."

"Maybe if I hadn't been distracted—"

Still staring at him, she made a tiny shocked sound. "Oh, my God. You're actually saying you're supposed to watch the entire ranch 24/7? That you can't take an evening off for yourself?"

Out of the corner of his eye, Cole saw Dutchy come out of the barn with Kyle. "This isn't the time or place." Cole pulled his gloves from his back pocket.

"My schedule is wide open. Tell me where and when." Her lips lifted in a teasing smile. "My room, tonight? If the ranch can spare you?"

He had to laugh. Persistent little thing. "You up for a ride, or are you still too sore?"

"Give me a minute to tell Rachel where I'm going." Jamie had already started backing toward the house.

"It won't be a joy ride," he called after her.

She smiled, turned and practically jogged the rest of the way to the front door, her shiny honey-colored hair bouncing off her slim shoulders.

Like a damn fool he stood there watching her instead of

getting busy and making sure the ATVs were gassed up. He knew he was courting trouble by taking her with him to Mill Creek Valley. Normally he wasn't one to speak first and think later. But something about Jamie was making him do all kinds of strange things. And what made everything worse, he had a feeling there wasn't a soul at the Sundance who didn't know it.

"YOU'RE SUCH A SOFTIE. I wonder if the men know," Jamie said, and smothered a laugh when she saw Cole grimace.

"Hell, they do now."

"Ouch." Her four-wheeler bounced over a particularly rough patch of earth, and every muscle in her backside screamed in protest.

She tugged down the tan hat she'd picked up in town, effectively keeping the sun out of her face, and stared at his taciturn profile. Even though she'd insisted she was fine to ride horseback, he'd stubbornly refused to listen. He'd chosen to take the ATVs, claiming that he often used one. A complete lie, she knew, because of the odd expressions on the faces of the men working in the corral as she and Cole rode past them.

"I think it's sweet that you're so concerned about my ass."

He gave her one of those single-arched-brow looks that he seemed able to summon at will. She envied him that, and had even practiced the look in front of the mirror, but couldn't get her eyebrow to cooperate.

When he returned his attention to the road ahead of them, she did, too, although she wished they'd only taken one four-wheeler instead of two. This way she couldn't lean in close to him and inhale his musky scent. Or wrap her arms around his waist. They rolled over another jarring bump, and she grunted at the pain.

"You okay?" His arm shot out protectively, even though he couldn't reach her.

"Fine." She noticed that the scarred tissue on his hand

seemed more vivid in the sunlight. "How did you get the scars?"

He shot her a confused look before noticing that she was staring at his hand. He flexed it, then made a fist. "They're from a long time ago."

"I can tell. You must've been a kid."

"Around eight."

She let up on the gas and slowed the ATV to a stop. He kept pace with her, exactly, all the while staring at her as if she'd gone off her rocker. But he didn't protest as she reached over, caught him by the wrist and placed his fist in her lap. He tensed a bit when she pried open his fingers but then he let her have her own way. She held back a smile at her little victory, but the grin died on its own as she studied his disfigured palm. "What happened?"

"A friend and I were playing where we shouldn't have been and he fell down an abandoned well."

She gasped. "Did he—was he—"

"It turned out okay. A ledge about eight feet down broke his fall. I found a rope and dropped it to him."

"Was it Noah?" She lightly traced one of the tracks with the tip of her finger.

"Nah, not that time." He laughed a little. "Lord knows we got in plenty of other trouble."

She shuddered, thinking about how horrible and raw the original wounds must have been to cause this much scarring. Unbidden, an image popped into her mind of Cole as a wiry boy, a rope wound tightly around his small hand as he struggled valiantly to lift his friend to safety. "Your friend was lucky you were there."

"I'm gonna need that."

"What?" She glanced up, saw him nod back at the trail and released his hand. They took off again, but they didn't go far.

While he steered them off the dirt road onto the grass, a dozen more questions filled her mind, but she sensed that he didn't want to talk about the incident anymore. She decided to leave it alone. Maybe he'd have more to say another time. For now she'd simply enjoy the beautiful country, the warm sunshine and, best of all, being alone with him.

No, the very best part was the fact that he'd asked her to come with him in the first place. She'd been so sure he was trying to put distance between them. This outing was far more than she'd hoped for.

"Any chance we'll be driving past a stream?" she asked.

"Thirsty?"

"I am."

"Hang on a minute." He led her toward a small grove of aspens and firs and made sure they both parked in the shade.

She didn't see a stream or creek, or even a mud hole for that matter. Then she watched him twist around and open the storage bin behind him. He pulled out a thermos and uncapped it.

"Ah, very clever." She laughed at herself. "You bring water with you."

"Yeah, an old cowboy trick." He smiled and watched her take a sip.

"What else have you got back there?"

"You'd be surprised."

"Go ahead, amaze and delight me."

With an amused expression, he turned off the engine.

"Good start," she murmured, her pulse quickening as she followed suit. There was lots of tall grass and tons of privacy all around them. Maybe he had a blanket stowed in the back.

He took the thermos from her, but didn't drink, just slowly screwed the cap back on.

She waited for him to do something, grew impatient and asked, "Is this the end of the road, so to speak? Where you'd intended to go before I barged in?"

"No, but I want to talk to you about Sadie's."

"The bar? Friday night? Rachel and I have it covered."

With a forefinger, he touched the brim of his hat, inching it back until he captured her gaze with his serious brown eyes. "I don't want you to go."

A frisson of unease shot down her spine. Mostly because she couldn't read him. "Why not? It's a good plan."

"If those boys get drunk enough to start talking, it should be to Josh and Kyle. Not you."

"The whole point is that they're more likely to talk to Rachel and me."

"This isn't your fight."

"I know," she said. "I offered to help."

His entire demeanor had changed. A tinge of resentment hardened his face and made her heart catch. He shifted and managed to put a few more inches between them. "Rachel was wrong in drawing you into a family matter."

Caught off guard, Jamie sat speechless. She was well aware she wasn't part of the McAllister clan. Did he think she was trying to worm her way inside his precious inner circle?

"Don't you leave Saturday?"

"Yes," she said, tersely. "What are you saying exactly? Do you think that because I'm staying on the same floor as you and Rachel and the rest of your family that I feel I'm entitled to overstep?"

He reared his head, his expression appearing to be one of genuine shock. "No."

It was too late. Hurt and embarrassment had gripped her. "Or do you think that because Rachel and I have gotten friendly, not to mention you and I getting down and dirty last night, that I'm trying to infiltrate your tight little group?" She paused to catch a badly needed breath.

"Jamie, no." He leaned across the short distance between the four-wheelers and caught her hand, his face a mask of confusion. "I can't even figure out what you're talking about. All I'm saying is that you don't wanna spend your last night at Sadie's."

She took a deep breath, felt a bit calmer. "Why not?"

He lightly squeezed her hand and hesitated. "I can't show up there. I hardly ever go to Sadie's. If they see me, Gunderson's boys will clam up."

"It seems you think the plan has merit, so I'm still not clear." She knew what she wanted to hear—that he'd like them to spend that last night together. But he'd have to admit it. She, apparently, was bad at drawing her own conclusions about him.

He lowered his gaze to her hand and traced a light pattern on her palm. "What if they're drunk and rowdy, and give you and Rachel a hard time?"

"Josh and Kyle would be there."

Cole stunned her by bringing her curled fingers to his lips, then brushed them across the skin above her knuckles. "Don't go."

"It's not only about me." Her hand trembled in his. "Rachel is involved."

"I'll talk to her." He leaned over, bracing one hand on her ATV. Her lips parted as he neared slowly until finally he kissed the corner of her mouth, then caught her lower lip with his teeth. The brims of their hats bumped, and she laughed shakily.

He drew away, whipping off his Stetson, and came back to her with more force, taking her mouth and persuasively using his tongue until she couldn't breathe.

If he were another man, she might have thought he was trying to play her, coax the answer from her that he wanted. Cole wasn't the type. He'd brought her out here because he wanted to be alone with her. Even though he'd tried to stay away he couldn't. The idea thrilled her to her core. Maybe he really did have a blanket back there....

The startling, unwelcome buzz of a ring tone broke the spell. She drew back and gazed dazedly at him. It wasn't her phone.

Cole muttered a mild oath, and gave her a small apologetic smile as he flipped open his cell. "Yeah," he said to the caller. "I'm five minutes away." He disconnected and exhaled sharply, staring bleakly at her. "I got two guys waiting for some gaskets." He nodded at the cargo bin. "Sorry."

"No problem." To be fair, he had told her it wasn't a joy ride.

Dammit. Right now, *fair* seemed overrated.

11

HOURS LATER JAMIE still didn't know what to think about the ride with Cole. Or the kiss. She refused to believe he'd been attempting to manipulate her, talk her out of going to Sadie's. No, not quite true. Despite her ego wanting to reject the idea, a small part of her understood that it was possible. For whatever reason, he didn't want her involved, and he might've rationalized his interference.

After all, she herself had been known to enlist the art of persuasion, so to speak. So expressing outrage, even to herself, was bogus. Still, she wished he hadn't ditched her as soon as they'd returned to the house after dropping off the gaskets.

He hadn't had dinner with Jamie and the rest of the guests, but that wasn't unusual. Most of the women were exhausted from rafting and hiking, so the meal was short, with minimal chatter, and that suited Jamie just fine.

After everyone scooted out of the dining room, leaving her and Rachel in peace, Jamie automatically started clearing the table. For the first time, Rachel didn't argue. Together they stacked the platters and plates, each making two trips to the kitchen. Hilda was gone. Rachel had chased her out as soon as the casseroles had been placed in the oven during cocktail hour on the porch.

Mrs. McAllister had helped serve the peach cobbler and coffee, then disappeared to take a phone call. Jamie glanced out the kitchen window. No sign of Cole. The question remained, should she bring up Sadie's, or would that be butting in too much? After all, Cole had said he wanted to talk to his sister.

The hell with it. Rachel and Jamie had put the plan together. If they decided to bag it, they needed to talk.

Rachel positioned herself at the sink. "You want to scrape and rinse, or load?"

Jamie hid a smile. "Doesn't matter. If you're fussy about how things go in the dishwasher, I don't mind scraping."

"Really?" Rachel said dryly. "You think I give a damn about how the dishes are loaded?"

"What was I thinking?" Jamie cut the grin loose. "Let me know if you see Cole out there, would you?"

"Sure. You went for an ATV ride with him earlier, huh?"

"Excuse me, but it wasn't a joy ride. Didn't you hear Cole announce it to all of west Montana before we left?" Jamie picked up a stack of rinsed plates, aware that Rachel was eyeing her with curiosity. "We took gaskets out to the men fixing the irrigation system."

Rachel burst out laughing.

Jamie looked over at her. "What?"

"I swear to God, my brother can be the most thick-headed man west of the Mississippi." She shook her head. "Don't get me wrong, he's a really good guy, but he's got these strange ideas about himself that make me want to just shake him sometimes."

Jamie pressed her lips together, hoping Rachel would elaborate without Jamie needing to prod. "Well…while we're on the subject…he feels strongly about us not going to Sadie's on Friday. He's planning on talking to you, but I figured I'd give you a heads-up."

"See, that's what I mean." Rachel's features tightened. She

didn't look happy, and already Jamie regretted butting in. "He thinks he should handle every little blip himself. That he's responsible for everything that goes wrong on this ranch."

"Oldest-brother syndrome?"

"That's part if it, I suppose." She stared out the window, her annoyance fading, replaced by a sadness that seemed to thicken the air. "It's more than that. There was an incident in his childhood. He was about eight...."

When it appeared that Rachel experienced a sudden loss of words, Jamie offered, "When his friend fell down the well?"

She turned to Jamie, and regarded her with wide-eyed shock. "He told you about that?"

Jamie swallowed; something that seemed kind of major was happening that she didn't understand. "I asked about the scars on his hands." She got rid of the plate she held and straightened. "Did I do something wrong by asking?"

Rachel looked past her. "You heard?"

Jamie abruptly turned. Mrs. McAllister had just entered the kitchen.

She nodded, her expression an odd mixture of concern and curiosity. Her gaze drifted from Jamie to Rachel and when it came back to Jamie, she saw a kindness in the woman's eyes that made Jamie's heart twist.

"I'm sorry, Mrs. McAllister, if I spoke out of turn."

The woman smiled. "First, I've already told you to call me Barbara, and you did nothing wrong." She moved closer and rubbed Jamie's arm. "Cole never talks about what happened, that's why we're surprised."

"Well, with those scars... I mean, people must know."

"Oh, everyone around here does. That's part of the problem, I suppose." Barbara shuddered and rubbed her own arms. "Lord, it happened so long ago, but even if he weren't my own son, the thought of any little boy, sitting out there for five hours, that rope wrapped so tightly that—"

Jamie blinked. "Five hours?"

Barbara stiffened and exchanged a glance with her daughter.

"I better stop you," Jamie said, her voice shaky. "Apparently he didn't tell me the whole story." She wanted to know the rest, desperately, but coming clean was the honorable thing to do. God, she hoped they ignored her confession.

"Let's all sit down and have a cup of coffee," Rachel said. "Okay, Mom?"

Jamie concentrated on loading glasses into the dishwasher, intent on giving the two women a modicum of privacy. If they were anything like Jamie and her friends, they could have an entire conversation with a few secret looks.

But when she couldn't stand the silence another second, she closed the dishwasher door and turned around, prepared to excuse herself.

Barbara had been watching her. A small pleased smile touched the corners of her mouth. "I believe you're right, Rachel. Time for coffee. Decaf okay with you, Jamie?" Barbara had already walked to the pantry and got out a black ceramic canister. "Or perhaps some tea?"

In that instant Jamie knew Rachel had discussed her with Barbara. What they found interesting to talk about was anyone's guess, but she was pretty sure she'd been the topic.

"Fine," she said, and noticed that Rachel had brought three pretty china cups out of the glass cabinet. "Either one."

Next the matching saucers came down, dainty and white, trimmed with gold. Very elegant, very scary. Jamie guessed the set had been passed down through generations and she did not want to be the one to break anything.

"Um, I'm normally not clumsy," she said, "but I'd prefer to stick to a mug."

Rachel grinned. "We trust you."

"Hope your faith isn't misplaced," Jamie murmured, her wary gaze following the china's trip to the kitchen table.

"The bad thing is these have to be hand-washed."

"Oh, for goodness sakes." With a laugh, Barbara measured out the coffee grounds. "I think I can handle that."

"I'll get the cream and sugar." Jamie had opened the refrigerator door before she realized her bad manners, and she gestured helplessly. "I hope you don't mind...."

"Right," Rachel said. "No help wanted in this kitchen."

Jamie smiled, but it wasn't her new friend she worried about offending. She didn't know her mother that well.

"I missed the peach cobbler," Barbara said. "Mind bringing the leftovers out, too?"

That easily, Jamie's concern was wiped clean, and within ten minutes they were all seated at the kitchen table, pigging out on Hilda's peach cobbler and strong coffee. Jamie prayed the conversation would be steered back to Cole and that day so long ago. That was the reason for this little powwow, she was pretty sure, but when it came to people and their motives, she'd been wrong plenty.

"It's nice to be able to use Great-Grandma's china," Barbara commented between bites. "We keep it under lock and key when the boys are around."

Jamie's cup was halfway to her lips, and she froze. "You had to remind me, didn't you?"

Barbara added more sugar to her coffee. "If it's survived my three little hellions, I suspect it's safe for another generation."

"That include Rachel?" Jamie asked.

"Hey, I thought you were my friend." She threw her wadded-up napkin, and Jamie ducked.

"It probably should have," Barbara agreed, giving her daughter a mock glare. "But she couldn't compete with her brothers in that department."

Jamie gave a snort of disbelief. "Not Cole."

"Yes, Cole." Barbara paused thoughtfully. "Until he was about fourteen. Though he was never as bad as Trace or Jesse for getting into trouble."

Rachel helped herself to another dollop of whipped cream. "I was too young to remember a time when Cole wasn't a straight arrow, what with eight years between us."

"And serious." Barbara sighed. "Always so sober, that one."

"What changed?" Jamie asked.

Neither woman seemed to mind her curiosity. Rachel looked to her mother to answer, and Barbara shrugged. "I personally think it started with Kenny falling into the well. Both he and Cole were normal mischievous little boys, and believe me, the final outcome could've been disastrous. The accident was traumatic for both boys. They probably needed some counseling, but we didn't understand that sort of thing back then."

"But Kenny is all right?" Jamie said in the form of a question, not so sure she wanted the answer.

"Oh, yeah." Rachel waved a hand. "Married and living in Butte with his wife and three kids." She got up, brought the carafe of coffee to the table and refilled their cups. "Mom, tell her the rest of the story."

Maybe Jamie had only imagined Barbara's hesitation, but in good conscience, she had to make the offer. "Want me to explain what he told me and then you decide what you want to fill in?"

Laughing, Rachel glanced at her mother. "Boy, you can tell *she's* not from around here."

"What?" Jamie's exasperation showed in spite of her efforts to keep it in check.

"Anyone else would've been leaning forward, all ears."

"Isn't that the truth?" Barbara sighed. "I appreciate your concern, Jamie, that was very thoughtful." She smiled. "It's not a big secret—nothing is around here—but I ask that you don't mention our conversation to Cole."

"Of course not."

"Good enough." Barbara took a sip of coffee. "The boys had been told a dozen times not to play around the abandoned property. Obviously they didn't listen. They were alone when Kenny fell in. He was fortunate to get tangled in some roots and ended up on a narrow ledge, or more like a few jutting rocks. An angel was sitting on his shoulder that afternoon, because it was a thirty-foot drop that could've killed him otherwise.

"Luckily, the boys had been practicing their lassoing so Cole had a rope. He dropped it to Kenny, told him to hang on and he'd pull him up. Cole couldn't do it. Kenny was on the chubby side and with him crying so hard, the only thing Cole could do was to get the boy to tie the rope around his waist so he wouldn't slip. Then Cole wrapped his end around his hand and waited for help. His voice was hoarse from yelling, and his small hands…" She briefly closed her eyes. "Dear God, they were so raw and bloody you could almost see bone by the time his father found him. He was convinced that if he let go for a second Kenny would die."

"So he stayed there holding the rope for five hours." Goose bumps had surfaced on Jamie's flesh and wouldn't subside. She didn't know much about normal eight-year-old behavior, but she'd been a year older when her parents had packed her off to Georgia, and she'd kicked and screamed like a baby.

Barbara nodded. "That was just like him, for all his troublemaking, he was loyal and true."

"The story spread like wildfire through the county," Rachel added. "I was still in diapers, but by the time I went to school, the story was still being told. Everyone kept saying, 'if there's one person you can count on it's Cole McAllister.' Nice sentiment, but not so much after it had been repeated a thousand times." She smiled sadly at her mother. "Honestly, I think that's why he's so anal about shouldering everything that happens on this ranch. It's that hyperactive sense of responsibility he can't shake."

"I can see that," Barbara said thoughtfully. "I also see him as that sad little boy who feels as if he failed."

"Failed?" Jamie finally found her voice again. "He was a hero."

"Not to Cole's mind, I'm afraid. He couldn't pull Kenny up and had to wait for help. By then both boys were dehydrated and bleeding. Sometimes I look at him—so serious, so filled with the need to protect us all—and I can see that little boy desperate to bring Kenny home."

Finding it difficult to swallow around the huge lump in her throat, Jamie brought the cup to her lips, hoping the liquid would help. All it did was remind her how much she hated lukewarm coffee, and she stared down at the offending brew.

"You're not eating your cobbler." Barbara touched her hand. "If we've upset you, I apologize."

"No." She concentrated on topping off her cup, not wanting them to see her moist eyes. "They didn't even have water?"

"They did, but Cole couldn't reach it without letting go of the rope. I swear, that boy still would've been hanging on twenty-four hours later if he'd had to. But fortunately it didn't come to that."

"Thank you for telling me the story." Jamie's voice broke. "Oh, God—I don't know why I'm acting so weird." She sniffed. "You'd think it had just happened."

"It's called empathy." Barbara cleared her throat and smiled as she reached for the carafe, clearly intending to change the subject. "Tell us about yourself, Jamie. Do you have a lot of brothers and sisters?"

"No, it's just me." She had the ridiculous urge to apologize. "My parents live abroad and are both quite involved in their careers."

"Oh, is that what gave you the traveling bug? Going to visit them?" Barbara asked. "Rachel told me you write a travel blog."

Jamie thought about lying, but what was the point? "I honestly don't see them all that much." She sighed. "They're very busy. But we email and talk…"

Surprise flitted across Barbara's face before she concealed it. Naturally a woman like her wouldn't understand. Her family meant everything to her.

"Good Lord, look what time it is." Rachel got up and peered out the window. "I should make Cole a thermos of coffee."

Jamie blinked. "Is he out there?"

"Not that I can see, but he should be along soon. He has the first watch." She shoved the curtain farther back. "Hmm, I hope it doesn't rain. Those clouds hovering over Mount Edith look pretty ominous."

"I heard we have a fifty-fifty chance of a scattered thunderstorm." Barbara started clearing the table.

Jamie hated thunder with a passion. Lightning she could abide, but the sound of thunder…at least it helped to know it might be coming. She realized she was still sitting there like a slug and jumped up to help Barbara. "What did you mean by 'he's taking the first watch'? Does that have to do with last night?"

Rachel nodded. "The men are taking shifts between sundown and sunup. It's just a precaution, and very low-key. I don't want the others to know."

"No, of course not." She put the stopper in the sink and grabbed the dish soap, and when both women looked at her with amusement, she said, "What?"

Barbara chuckled. "I have a feeling it wouldn't do any good to insist I take over."

"You're right." Grinning, Jamie took the plates from her.

"Then I believe I'll go upstairs and catch up on some reading." Barbara surprised Jamie with a one-armed hug around her shoulders. "If you ever find yourself at loose ends during the holidays you're always welcome here."

"Not as a paying guest," Rachel said, laughing.

"Good heavens, no." Barbara flushed. "I meant as our personal guest."

"I may take you up on the offer sometime. Thank you," Jamie said quietly, touched by the woman's kindness. Though she doubted she'd ever actually accept, not unless Cole did the inviting.

"She really likes you," Rachel said after her mother left. "Holidays are sacred to her. It doesn't seem to matter that all us kids are in her face every day. She likes having the family around her and observing traditions at Thanksgiving and Christmas. Her offer was sincere. I hope you take it seriously."

"I do. Frankly, I'm honored, though she barely knows me. Guess I've been butting in too much."

Rachel smiled absently, her expression betraying her faraway thoughts. "You and I are a lot alike. I think she sees that." The coffeemaker made a weird burping noise signaling the end of its task. "This should be ready in a minute, mind taking the thermos out to Cole?"

"Did you see him?" Jamie moved to the window.

"No, but it's getting dark so I know he's out there. No way he'd miss his shift."

Jamie unscrewed the thermos lid and reached for the coffeepot. "He doesn't know it yet, but he's going to have company."

"I had a feeling...."

"God, am I that sickeningly obvious?"

"Pretty sure only to me," Rachel said, then laughed when Jamie groaned.

COLE STOOD AT THE entrance to the barn and stared at the well-lit house with a feeling in his gut that was part relief and part disappointment. Jamie's room was dark, which he assumed meant she was downstairs. He should've gone inside instead of grabbing a quick sandwich with Dutchy and Chester in the bunkhouse. Jamie probably thought he was avoiding her. To some extent he was.

All his life he'd prided himself on his self-control and good sense. Around her, it seemed, he possessed neither. And it was a hell of a time not to have his head screwed on straight. If the economy wasn't enough to run the Sundance into the ground, the new rash of thefts might be the icing on the cake. His hope was that whoever was behind the thievery had moved on. Not a particularly charitable thought since that could mean another rancher would suffer.

He heard the kitchen door creak, reminded himself to oil the hinges and peered into the gathering darkness. Only the usual low overnight lights had been left on. No need to change routine and alert anyone who might have been watching the place.

With the thick cloud covering it was darker than usual for the hour, but even in the dimness he recognized Jamie's silhouette. How was it possible that he'd known her only a few days? How could he want her so damn much that it threw him off track? Made him forget that his first responsibility was to the Sundance and his family? That it would always be that way for him?

What was it about her, dammit? Was it that lurking vulnerability she tried so hard to hide? On the surface she seemed to have it all. At least that's what she'd have everyone believe. Behind the carefree smile and easy sophistication, there was a vulnerability that tugged at his heart. He didn't quite understand it yet. Probably never would. She wasn't the type of woman who stuck around for long.

Jamie started to veer toward the stables then stopped, he suspected to allow her eyes to grow accustomed to the dimness.

"Over here," he said, moving into view. Her timing was good. It was too early for any trouble so he didn't worry about being seen.

She headed toward him, her lips lifting in a cheeky grin. "What makes you think I'm looking for you?"

He waited until she reached him, then drew her back into

the shadows inside the barn. Cole took the thermos from her, set it on the railing and nudged up her chin. Those damn kiss-able lips. He knew too well how soft they were. "Then tell me, Jamie, what are you looking for?"

12

HE'D STARTLED HER with the question. And with the way he'd caught her arm and pulled her close, right out in the open where anyone could see them. Admittedly, the light was murky and a person could assume he simply didn't want either of them to be seen by a thief casing the place.

She made no such assumption—she knew better. And not only because of the way he absently stroked her arm or how he brushed the back of his hand along her jaw. A spark had ignited between them and she had the sudden and distinct feeling that this was the night for fireworks. The only question was when.

"Oh, I get it," she said finally. "You're trying to distract me."

"From?"

"Telling you that I'm going to help you keep watch."

He lowered both hands, his expression turning flat. "No, you're not."

"I am. Rachel thinks it's an excellent idea."

He shot a frown toward the kitchen. "I don't care. You have five minutes, then you're marching right back into that house."

She wasn't about to let him get away with pulling back. Not to mention she didn't care for his bossiness. "You're such a coward."

"Let's put it this way…" He gave her the arched brow. This time, however, he looked more arrogant than amused. "How much *watching* do you think we'd get done?"

"Wow, progress." Impressed that he hadn't pretended disinterest, she flattened a palm on his chest. His heart pounded as hard as hers. "Sadly, I see your point. But no, I will not be a good little girl and do as you've so charmingly ordered."

"It wasn't an order," he muttered. "It was a strongly worded request. I know you understand that I have to stay alert out here."

"Correct. That's why we'll behave like adults and refrain from making out."

"Making out," he repeated with a snort. "Haven't heard that term in a while." Then he caught her wrist and pulled her hand away from his chest. "Not a good start."

Muted light from the house shone onto his face. The desire she saw in his sexy brown eyes made her pulse race like crazy. "I'm rethinking this. Are you officially on watch yet?" She moved so that her breasts rubbed against him. "Come on, you started this."

He opened his mouth as if to object, then shut it again.

She laughed softly. "It's barely dark. No one would be stupid enough to try and sneak in now. I promise that once we seriously need to pay attention, I'll be as good as gold. But I figure we have at least an hour."

"For?"

"Oh, I don't know…" With the tip of her finger she traced his lower lip. "Nothing requiring us to get naked. Too risky. Just some kissing, and maybe I'll even let you get to first base."

Cole laughed. It was a really good laugh, one she hadn't heard before. "What exactly does that mean?"

"Huh." That stopped her. "I'm not sure."

He cupped her breast. "This maybe?"

Shocked, she sucked in a breath. It would've been better if

he'd reached under her shirt, but still… "I think you're getting warm." She exhaled slowly. "At least I am," she murmured when he rubbed her taut nipple with his thumb.

"See?" he whispered, his lips warm and moist against the skin below her ear. "This is what I was trying to avoid." He found her earlobe with his teeth and tugged lightly. "I can't do this, Jamie, not now."

"I'm not forcing you." Her voice broke when he slipped his other hand under her knit top.

He splayed his fingers over her ribcage, stilled for a moment, then held her by her waist and covered her mouth with his. She slid her arms around his neck, and pressed her breast against his palm. He deepened the kiss, plunging his tongue into her willing mouth.

She deserved this agony. In teasing him, her own desire had sparked and raged like wildfire in her belly even though she knew it couldn't lead to anything. She moved her hips against his, and found him so hard it made her ache with longing. His groan swept the inside of her mouth, vibrated in her chest and pooled like liquid heat between her thighs.

Seconds later she sensed his withdrawal even before he moved his head back and broke the intensity of the kiss. His lips grazed hers, and then he brushed them back and forth. If he was trying for a cool-down, he'd missed the mark. She only wanted more. But then he lowered his hands and smoothed her shirt.

"I'm sorry," she whispered. "I didn't mean to get carried away."

He smiled against her mouth and caught her hand. Unprepared, she gasped when he pressed her palm against his bulging fly.

"Like this?" His low gravelly voice did amazing things to her ultra-sensitive breasts. As if he understood the ache he'd inspired, he lowered his head and drew a puckered nipple into his mouth. Moist heat penetrated her thin shirt and bra, proving they were a token barrier.

"Cole, this is…oh, God." She whimpered when he used his teeth.

"This is what?" he murmured, and she didn't miss the hint of amusement in his voice.

"War." She dragged her palm down his fly and cupped him at the base.

He bit off a curse that she somehow found immensely satisfying, until he lifted his head and said, "This is why you can't stay out here."

She moved her hand. "Okay, I get it. Paws off for now." At this point, she knew she was doomed to a long frustrated night, and vaguely wondered what it would take for him to swap shifts with the guy who was supposed to relieve him. But if she suggested it, he'd probably send her back into the house for sure. "But that means you, too."

"Right." His hand trailed away from her waist, one last brush of his fingertips across her midriff, his obvious reluctance making her hot again.

She took a deep shuddering breath. "And you're sharing your coffee with me." Although some ice-cold water sounded pretty good about now. Two tall glasses. One to gulp down, the other to douse herself with.

His teeth gleamed white in the dimness. "Yes, ma'am."

She noticed that he'd already set up a folding camp-style chair. "And I'll need one of those," she said, pointing, then noticed the rifle propped against the wall. It gave her the creeps. "I'm not standing all night…. How long is your shift, anyway?"

"Four hours."

She did a quick mental calculation. "So we're talking about one-thirty. Okay," she said, nodding.

"Glad you approve."

"I don't. You won't get any sleep tonight."

"No?"

She paused. "Maybe an hour."

He chuckled. "Ambitious little thing, aren't you?"

"I'd prove it but we agreed we wouldn't do that yet."

"Christ," Cole muttered, and walked to the small window, facing north. He pretended to check the driveway, but she could tell he was adjusting his fly.

Her gaze went back to the rifle. "Would you actually use that thing?"

He turned. "The Ruger? If I had to."

"Have you ever…?"

"I've shot my share of wolves and coyotes that were attacking the cattle."

"Oh, of course. Do you hunt?" She tried to keep the censure out of her voice. She understood the culture, still hated the idea of it, though. "I imagine that's a common sport around here."

"Hunting should never be considered a sport. If you need the meat to feed your family, that's different." He moved the chair away from the wall. "Here. I won't be doing much sitting."

She suddenly realized that he was wearing all-dark clothes, probably to enable him to move freely without being seen. While the jeans she wore were appropriate, she glanced down in dismay at her pale pink top.

"Should I change?" She brought her head up and caught movement out of the corner of her eye.

She shot a look in that direction and wondered if the looming shadows had been playing tricks on her. Then she saw them, a pair of gold glowing eyes. She covered her mouth to stifle a scream, but jumped a good two feet.

"What's wrong?"

"I saw something—someone's in there." She pointed, her arm shaking. "Or something."

Cole pulled a flashlight out of his back pocket and shone

the beam at the far end of the barn. A big charcoal-gray cat walked lazily along the top of the railing that ran under the hayloft, its bushy tail twitching.

"Oh, hell, that's just Luther."

At the sound of his name, the cat peered over his shoulder at them, and then dismissively swished his tail before leaping onto a hay bale.

"He's huge." Jamie's laugh was high, nervous and annoying to her own ears. "Sorry for the false alarm."

"Not as big as his brother." Cole swept the beam of light from floor to ceiling. "Blue's around somewhere. They stick close to the barn. Antisocial little devils, but they're both good mousers."

"You mean, they catch and eat mice."

"That's their job."

"Eew."

He smiled. "You'd rather have a bunch of field mice scurrying over your feet?"

She groaned, peering uneasily down at the floor and imagining all things creepy-crawly slithering across the toes of her boots. "Thank you for that," she said, her voice dripping with sarcasm.

He chuckled. "Every critter has a job on this ranch. Now make yourself useful and pour us some coffee."

"Oh, how far we've come," she muttered, sitting on the chair and clamping the thermos between her thighs while she unscrewed the cap. "I'm surprised you don't have a couple of guard dogs."

"We did. Not a guard dog. We've never had a problem with thefts around here before. Buster was a pet, part border collie, part shepherd. We had him for fourteen years. He's buried behind the house under that grove of aspens. His favorite shady spot on a hot afternoon."

"I'm sorry."

"That's the way of things," he said, shrugging, and took

the cup she offered him. "We'll end up getting another dog, but it's only been seven months. I don't think either Rachel or Trace is quite ready to take in a replacement." He sipped the coffee and gazed idly toward the door.

Not for a second did she believe he'd been less affected than his siblings over the loss of their pet. He could put up the toughest front he wanted, but she sensed his grief. Even heard the sadness in his voice and saw it in the slump of his shoulders. Fourteen years was a long time to love someone or something and have it taken away.

"I always wanted to have a dog, or even a cat. Mostly a dog, though, a medium-size one would've been nice so she could sleep with me but still go for long walks." She glanced toward the back. "No offense, Luther and Blue."

"Arrogant beasts. They wouldn't give a damn even if they did understand you." He moved to pass the thermos cup back to her. "Sorry, you want some?"

She shook her head. "Not yet, I just had decaf with your mom and Rachel. You missed some awesome peach cobbler."

"There better be leftovers."

"Nope. I polished it off. You missed dinner, so too bad."

Cole smiled at her. Time seemed to freeze as they looked into each other's eyes. He lifted his hand, and for a second she thought he was going to touch her. But then he plowed his fingers through his dark hair and turned to study something outside the barn doors.

After a stretch of silence, he asked, "Why didn't you have a pet?"

"Actually, I did. Two goldfish. Oh, and a turtle when I was about five. Want me to top off your coffee?"

He shook his head. "I meant real pets."

"Hey, they had names. They were real." She set the thermos aside and got to her feet. He was studying her now, his intense dark eyes almost daring her to be flip. "We moved a lot. A dog or cat would've been too much of a hassle."

"What about later? When you were on your own?"

"Same problem. I travel an average of two weeks out of the month. It wouldn't be fair." She turned away when he kept looking at her as if she'd skimped on the answer. "Maybe someday when I get tired of writing the blog I'll find an animal shelter and fall madly in love." Self-conscious, she laughed. "I meant with an animal...you know...that I found at the shelter."

"Don't even walk into one of those places until you're ready. Hard to leave empty-handed."

"I know." Jamie sighed. "I'll have to make sure someone goes with me, armed with handcuffs and duct tape."

"Duct tape?"

She gave him her best smile. "I can be very persuasive."

He rubbed the back of his neck, a grin threatening the corners of his mouth. "That's a fact."

Delighted with his boyish expression, Jamie laughed. "You are so lucky we're in the middle of a truce, or I'd eat you up."

Cole snorted, a stunned look giving way to a groan. "You are truly something else."

"I like to think so."

He tossed the last few drops of his coffee onto the floor and then crouched to pick up the thermos. "Any ideas what else you'd do after the blog?"

"Frankly, I haven't thought that far ahead. The blog has been ridiculously profitable." She watched him screw the top on, his hands in the perfect spot to catch the muted light. If she didn't know about the scars they might not have been noticeable.

She wished he'd been the one to tell her the details of that long-ago day. Unfortunately she couldn't think of a way to bring it up without betraying Rachel and Barbara's confidence.

"I reckon you never get tired of traveling, so no reason to look for something else."

"Oh, I get plenty tired at times." She stretched her arms over her head, arching her back, surprised at the tension she was holding. "Airport security can be aggravating as hell, and then no matter how well I research a hotel beforehand, sometimes I get there and want to pull my hair out. I never mind roughing it, but I want to know ahead of time." She sighed. "Naturally in my blog I make everything sound like an adventure or make it funny. But that gets old, too."

She hesitated. "I like your mom. We had a nice chat over coffee before I came out here." Jamie cleared her throat, hoped she wasn't about to make a huge mistake. Without being too obvious, she slid a peek his way. "She even invited me to come back for the holidays."

"She did?"

"She knows my parents live abroad and I don't have siblings," Jamie added quickly. "So she figured I might be on my own. Which I'm not usually, and if I am I don't care.... Holidays have never been that big a deal...." She sighed at the stricken look on his face. Why hadn't she kept her big mouth shut? He probably figured next she'd suggest she move into his room, and they hadn't even had sex yet. She hoped she hadn't just squashed her chance.

He didn't say a word, just stared. And okay, maybe he hadn't looked stricken exactly, more surprised. Whatever he'd been feeling, he recovered. No way to guess what he was thinking now. His face was a perfect blank, which further grated on her nerves.

"I'd never impose... Holidays are for family...." Her throat seemed to be blocked again and she fiercely worked at trying to clear it. "I just thought it was nice of her to offer," she finished lamely.

"You wouldn't be an imposition. I know my mother, and that invitation wasn't extended lightly."

"That's sort of what Rachel said. Still, I seriously doubt

I would take her up on it." A thought occurred to her. "Are you guys going to be open during Christmas?"

"Hell, I hope not." He clearly realized that might not have been the appropriate response and winced. "We haven't talked about it. I say no, but I reckon Rachel will get her way."

"I was just wondering. If you wanted the business, I wouldn't mind pimping the place on my blog."

"Pimping?"

She rolled her eyes. "It's a common term."

"In the city, maybe."

"Everywhere."

A wry resignation touched the corners of his mouth, and he checked his watch. "Time to lie low and keep our ears open."

Stuffing her hands in her pockets, she hunched her shoulders. "Are you really expecting trouble?"

"It's unlikely they'd hit the same ranch twice. Noah and I agree on that, but, like he says, if they're slick and experienced, they might anticipate our expectation and do otherwise."

"Noah used to be a city cop, right?"

"Yep. In Chicago."

"But he came back," she said quietly, mostly to herself. "Just like Rachel."

"So far."

She turned and stared. "You don't think she'll stay?"

"No telling. Not much here for a bright young woman." He felt his back pocket as if to assure himself he still had his flashlight and then fiddled with the switch near the door, dimming the already muted flat lights installed where the ceiling met the walls. "Be sure to stay back from the light coming from the house."

In the past few minutes he'd grown restless, pacing to each of the six windows and squinting into the darkness. She wished she could see his face better because there had been an odd quality to his voice she didn't understand. Had there been a message for her in his words? Or was she being too self-absorbed? Most likely he'd been talking strictly about his sister and hadn't given Jamie a thought.

"I wouldn't mind it if that storm cut loose," he said, looking out the back window toward the mountains.

"Oh, God, why?"

"We could use the rain."

"But not the thunder and lightning."

"Not the lightning," he agreed. "We've had enough wild-fires this month. The BLM people are still monitoring one of the burns. It's already cleared out over three hundred acres. I understand why. Still makes me nervous."

"BLM," she repeated. "I should know what that means."

"Bureau of Land Management."

"Okay, so maybe I didn't know what that meant. Not much government land in the city."

"No, I expect not." He cocked his head. "Hear that?"

"What?"

"Thunder. Not close. Over toward Big Belt Mountains."

Jamie wrapped her arms around herself, glad she hadn't heard the boom, and wishing he hadn't pointed it out. No, it was better to be prepared.

"You cold?" He came to her, taking her by the shoulders and then skimming his palms down her warm skin.

She drew in a deep breath. "I hate thunder."

He smiled at her as if she were a frightened child. "Thunder won't hurt you."

"I know that," she snapped, then felt appalled that she'd nearly taken his head off. "Sorry. It's one of those irrational fears," she muttered.

He frowned, not angry, but concerned. "Maybe you should go back to the house."

"No, that's silly. I'm fine." She pulled away, and rubbed her hands down the front of her jeans.

Lightning flashed, momentarily lighting up the inside of

the barn. One of the cats took a startled leap from a bale of hay onto the dirt floor and darted for cover.

Jamie gasped, knew the clap of thunder was seconds away.

The warning didn't help at all. When the earth-shattering boom split the silence, she covered her ears. It didn't make a bit of difference. She was already shaking. No amount of reasoning with herself ever erased that long-ago day.

13

COLE SIMPLY STARED at Jamie. At first he'd thought she'd been teasing him about being afraid of the thunder. But when he saw that she was trying hard, but unsuccessfully, to calm herself, he slid his arms around her.

She started to fight him but he refused to release her. He pulled her trembling body against his chest and rubbed her back. He didn't say anything, because hell if he knew what to say. Instead he kissed the top of her head and hugged her tighter when she buried her face against his shoulder.

Another bolt of lightning flashed close, and he knew the whole damn barn was about to shake. He hunched over her, hoping he could block out some of the sound but of course it was useless. The loud rumble roared over them like a stampede of panicked mustangs.

Jamie went so still it actually scared him. Then she whimpered. That was it. He was taking her inside the house and giving her a shot of whiskey to calm her nerves. After that... shit, he didn't know, but he wouldn't leave her alone. Not like this.

She moved, and this time when he tried to hold her tighter, she struggled to free herself. Abruptly she stumbled backward and caught his biceps. He didn't try to pull her back in, just made sure she had a firm grip of his arm.

"I'm okay," she said breathlessly. "Mortified, but I'll survive."

"No reason to be embarrassed."

With a nervous laugh, she released him and shoved the tangled hair away from her face. Except the strands clung stubbornly to her pale cheeks, and he noticed then they were damp with tears. "You have some doozies out here." Her wary gaze went toward the window. "How long do these storms normally last?"

"Hard to say."

She gave him a wan smile. "You could've lied."

"Come here." A slight tug of her hand and she was back in his arms. "We're all afraid of something," he whispered against her hair. "No need to feel ashamed."

"It's not that I'm afraid," she said, then sighed heavily. "The first sound is the worst. I have a physical reaction I can't seem to control, then I settle down fairly quickly. I'm pretty sure it's some weird psychosomatic crap left over from childhood."

He shouldn't be enjoying the feel of her slim body pressed against his. Not when he felt the thrum of a slight tremor down her spine. Though oddly she did seem calmer, even when another thunder clap echoed from the distance. "Has it always been like this?"

"No." She hesitated, and he got the feeling that she understood the trigger for her reaction. But he wouldn't press. Everyone had secrets they kept close to the vest.

He rested his chin on top of her head, content to feel her heartbeat strong and steady against his chest. "How about we go in the house?"

She pulled back and stared up at him. "No. You're on watch."

He shrugged. "This kind of weather…I doubt anyone has it in their head to go prowling tonight."

"Why not? The storm is the perfect distraction."

"People are more alert. Not tucked in their beds asleep."

"Well, I suppose that makes sense, but we're not going in on my account."

Cole smiled at the obstinate lift of her chin. The next loud roar might wring some of the starch out of her. He touched that stubborn chin, then let his fingers trail over her throat, down the front of her shirt. "Inside could be far more interesting."

She shivered, then laughed. "That wasn't from the thunder," she said.

Lightning flashed again. Their gazes met and locked. They both knew what came next. No need to point it out. He opened his arms, and she pressed her body against his just as the sky exploded like a bomb.

He briefly closed his eyes and held her tighter. It was kind of eerie how well she fit, how right she felt snuggled against him. He wasn't the type who easily let someone close. He was friendly enough, as hospitable as the next man, but in a small community like Blackfoot Falls, a person had to be careful if they valued their reputation.

With Jamie, caution seemed to slip from him like a greased pig at the county fair. The woman kept surprising him. She was strong, independent and full of opinions, yet mindful not to cross the line or treat people as if they were a bunch of hicks simply because they chose to live in a narrower, more black-and-white world. She didn't overlook people or view them as novelties just because they were different, and she wouldn't be sticking around.

He'd sooner have a shotgun put to his ribs than admit it, but his ideals were too old-fashioned to appreciate most of the city women who were guests at the ranch. They bewildered him, and sometimes left him downright cold. Maybe his attitude had to do with Bella and how much she'd changed after leaving Blackfoot Falls to make her mark in the world. Every time she returned, it seemed they had less to talk about and the sex wasn't as good.

Hell, not that he'd turned her down even once. He had needs. She always seemed to have an itch. And for the week or two that she was home, it worked out okay for both of them.

But when it came to Jamie, it wasn't just Cole...even his mother knew she was different. Inviting her to share the holidays with them was a monumental gesture. As generous a woman as Barbara McAllister was, she could be out-and-out stingy when it came to preserving private family traditions. Rachel had never missed a Thanksgiving or Christmas, and when Jesse had been deployed for those two years, the holidays had been too somber.

It finally occurred to him that Jamie wasn't shaking so much. He loosened his hold, and she looked up at him. Her face wasn't as pale as before but the sparkle in her eyes wasn't back yet.

He lowered his head and lightly kissed her soft lips. "You okay?"

"Much better." She smiled. "Kissing always makes it better."

Keeping a straight face, he narrowed his eyes. "Was this whole thing an act?"

"I wish." She sniffed. "It's not just thunder, I hate any loud noise I'm not expecting." After a long thoughtful moment, she said, "When I was nine, the embassy in Bosnia where my parents worked was attacked. The violence was unexpected, and when the bombs went off, everyone went nuts. It was utter chaos."

"Jesus, were you hurt?"

"No, no, nothing like that. I was in school with the rest of the American kids. We were within the walls of the compound though, away from the gunfire and explosions, but we didn't know what was happening. That was the worst part."

"What about your parents?" he asked, dreading her answer. They were alive, he reminded himself. Living in Europe, he was pretty sure she'd said.

"They'd been evacuated immediately. My father was high on the food chain, a valuable asset, so they were protected," she said with a touch of cynicism. "So was I. A guard pulled me away from my classmates and the next thing I knew I was sitting in a military plane headed for the States."

"By yourself?"

"Four other kids had been packed up, too. All of us close to the same age, none of us knew what was going on. After we landed in D.C. I was transferred to a commercial flight to Georgia, where my uncle and aunt took me to live on their peanut farm, south of Atlanta." She stared at a spot on his shirt. "I'd only met them and my cousin once before. They were practically strangers to me. I ended up living with them for three years, and now my cousin Kaylee and I are really great friends."

"Did you see your parents before you left Bosnia?"

"I saw my mother briefly, not my father, though. They came to visit me six months later."

"Three years was a long time to be separated from them." He didn't like that she seemed to have trouble looking him in the eye, almost as if she was embarrassed. It didn't make sense. "At least you were with family."

"I guess." She sighed. "My parents could've sent for me when they were transferred to Greece a year later, but I think they got used to being childless." Her gaze darted to his face and she flushed. "That makes them sound like horrible people, but they aren't."

"The thought never crossed my mind," he assured her, not that he understood how they could've abandoned their daughter. Even he could see years later how much she'd been affected by the ordeal.

She moved back until she was out of reach. "Duty to country is way up there on the old priority list. Gotta respect their dedication," she said, and, hugging herself, frowned toward the window. "Still no rain, huh?"

Watching her, he felt helpless and uneasy, because he knew she wasn't okay in spite of the brave front. She was lonely. He'd seen it in her eyes and heard the proof in her voice a couple days ago. He simply hadn't been able to identify what was going on at the time.

"Don't they have counselors for kids who've experienced traumas?" he asked, and she turned to glare at him. Hell, he should've kept his mouth shut. "I don't know anything about that sort of thing…I was just saying—"

"I have nothing against therapy—for those who need it. It wasn't as if I suffered from post-traumatic stress." She squared her shoulders. "If I'd needed counseling, my parents would've seen to it. They aren't monsters."

"Jamie, come on."

"Oh, God, I'm sorry. I know you didn't mean anything."

Frustrated, he picked up the thermos, left the chair as it was, and grabbed the rifle. "We're going in the house."

The barn lit up as if someone had flipped on a switch. He shot a look through the window and saw a second bolt of jagged lightning streak through the black storm clouds. Damn, it was close. Too close. His gaze swung back to Jamie. With fists clenched and lips pressed tightly together, as though mentally bracing herself, she stared back at him.

She still flinched when the sky bellowed. "I appreciate what you're trying to do, but going inside won't change anything."

"Humor me."

Shouting from outside made him freeze, his gut twist. The

yells were coming from the bunkhouse. He dropped the thermos, but held on to the rifle and ran outside.

Josh and Kyle dashed toward him.

"Fire!" Josh called. "On the west side."

"Lightning," Kyle added as both men rushed past Cole to
get to the water wagon.

In various stages of undress, the men poured out of the
bunkhouse and ran for their gear.

"Cole, what can I do?"

He turned to Jamie and saw the fire's glow over the roof of
the stables. A tree near the ridge had gone up in flames, fortunately far enough from the outer buildings that they could
stop it before the blaze did any real damage. "Nothing. Get
in the house. The men all know what to do."

"I can help."

"You'll only be in the way. I'm serious, Jamie, get inside,"
he called over his shoulder as he headed for a four-wheeler.
"Call Trace out here. Tell Rachel what's going on and that
everything is under control."

Dammit, he hoped Jamie did what she was told. He didn't
need to worry about her on top of getting that fire put out.
The heavy humid air already smelled of smoke—overhead
the black rain-swollen clouds stubbornly hoarded moisture
like a bloated, dammed river. They needed a good down-
pour about now.

Cole jumped onto the four-wheeler and, in spite of himself,
glanced toward the front door of the house. Good. Jamie had
disappeared. He hoped she'd found Trace and Rachel. Neither one would let her outside to get into trouble. Rachel for
sure would encourage her to stay put. Better for everyone.
Especially for Jamie.

And him.

He reached for the key that was no longer in the ignition
and cursed a blue streak. After the theft, they'd decided not
to leave keys in any of the vehicles. It took him a moment

to remember that the key had been moved to just under the left back wheel well. He found it, and was about to start her up when he saw Jesse's Jeep rambling down the driveway. Good timing.

Five guys manning the water wagon took off for the ridge, and Cole waited for Jesse. By the time Jesse pulled up alongside Cole on the ATV, Trace ran outside. Foregoing the porch steps, he jumped to the ground.

The screen door that had just slammed behind him flew open.

"Son of a bitch," Cole muttered, when Jamie and Rachel came running out.

AN HOUR AND A HALF LATER when the rain finally cut loose, water came down in buckets. Cheers erupted from the weary men on the front line. Everyone else echoed sighs of relief.

Dutchy clapped Lucas on the shoulder, apparently forgetting for the moment that he'd earlier accused the wrangler of cheating at Texas Hold 'em.

Jesse briskly herded the men back to the business of squelching the fire for good. The rain helped ensure they wouldn't be breaking their backs for another two hours, but everyone knew an overlooked smoldering ember could reignite the whole ridge as soon as it was dry again.

The fire had covered a far wider area than Cole had anticipated. Four trees had gone up in flames, a quarter acre of shrubs were nothing but skeletons and ash and the ground was mostly black but for the occasional orange glow. Still, they'd gotten off easy. If things had gone sideways and the fire had cut a path toward the ranch...

Hell, Cole couldn't even think about that.

Instead, he eyed Jamie. She stood off to the side by herself, her face turned up to the rain, her eyelids shut tight, exhaustion bracketing her mouth. On the one hand he wanted to kill her for disobeying orders, and on the other, he wanted to throw her over his shoulder and cart her back to the house while kissing every inch of her brave little ass.

Damn, he couldn't believe how she'd stepped in and carried heavy buckets of water, for the most part keeping up with the men. As much as she'd pissed him off, he respected and admired her for her gumption. The lightning and thunder hadn't quit until half an hour ago, and she'd been shaking like a leaf at times, but she'd never missed a step. She'd faced her fear and spat in its eye.

"Don't you dare utter a cross word to her." Rachel had come to stand beside him, and she too squinted through the rain to watch Jamie.

"You're the one I'm pissed at," Cole said, flexing his taut shoulder muscles. "Why the hell didn't you both stay in the damn house? You know better."

"Like we weren't a big help." Grimacing, Rachel pushed her wet hair back and twisted it into a soppy ponytail. "I like her. A lot."

He hesitated. "Me, too."

A slow grin stretched across his sister's face and she leaned against him. "Good for you for admitting it. Mom likes her, too. She invited her for the holidays, if you can believe that."

"Think she'll come?"

"I don't know. Maybe if we pushed. Don't ask me why, but I get the impression she's lonely." Rachel's shared observation sliced through him. "How would you feel about her being here?"

He didn't know how to answer that, but he was saved from having to do so by Jamie.

She brought her head up and vigorously wiped her waterlogged face, her wry, what-the-hell-am-I-doing expression making them both laugh.

Rachel sighed. "I'm done. I'm going back to the house with anyone who'll give me a ride."

"Get in Jesse's Jeep. I'll tell him to take both of you back."

He doesn't need to stay out here, either. I think he flew back from Idaho. He has to be beat."

"I don't know…" Rachel batted at the rain as if it would do any good. "He won't like me getting his seats wet."

"He'll get over it." Cole spotted his brother crouched over a patch of charred ground, inspecting a dying ember. "I'll get him, you get Jamie."

Rachel caught Cole's arm. "She won't go back without you."

"That's crazy."

She gave a small shrug. "Maybe, but I'm telling you, she won't leave."

Snorting, he veered off toward Jamie. "I'm gonna get Jesse," he said to her as if the matter were settled. "You and Rachel can get a ride with him to the house."

Using her hand like a visor, Jamie shielded her eyes from the rain. "You, too?"

"No."

"Okay, I can wait."

"Look, I wasn't happy you showed up to begin with—"

"Yeah, so?" With a complete lack of concern, she blinked.

"If I have to carry you to that Jeep, don't think I won't," he said through gritted teeth. He almost glanced at Rachel but stopped himself. No doubt she was enjoying this.

Jamie laughed. "Right." She tilted her head back and scowled at the sky. "The rain is slowing down. Is that bad? Was it enough?"

Cole cursed. "This is not the time to be stubborn," he said in a low warning voice.

She switched her focus to him, her eyebrows arching in amusement. "When have I ever listened to you?"

"All right." He clenched his jaw so tightly that his temples throbbed as he walked over to Jesse. "Can I borrow your Jeep? I'll be right back."

"Sure." Jesse's puzzled frown shot to Rachel, then Jamie.

"You don't have to come back. Everything's under control here. I'll take the four-wheeler when we're done."

"I'll be back." Something in his voice must've stirred the pot, because several pairs of eyes turned to him.

Dutchy even set down a bucket and watched with unabashed curiosity as Cole did an about-face and headed for Jamie.

"Last chance," he told her. "You gonna climb into that Jeep?"

"No," she said flatly.

He didn't say another word until he opened the passenger door, checked to make sure the keys were in the ignition, then rounded the hood. "Remember," he said, "you asked for this."

Jamie grinned. "Ooh, you're getting all caveman on me. I think I like it."

Tension had been steadily building in his gut and his struggle for restraint slipped. Why the hell couldn't she for once do as she was told? This wasn't fun and games. Vaguely aware he had an audience, he wrapped his arms around her waist and threw her over his shoulder.

She let out a startled shriek. "What are you doing?" she asked, and started laughing.

So did the men, first in nervous surprise, then in loud uproarious chortles.

Making sure he had a firm grip, he tightened his hold around her thighs before retracing his path on the rocky ground to the other side of the Jeep.

Her breasts bounced against his back with every uneven step he took. "Hey." She squirmed, and then smacked his ass.

He returned the favor, with an open hand to her nicely curved backside. She only laughed again. A sudden wave of pure healthy lust swept over him, and then he caught a glimpse of Rachel's open-mouthed stare. Bad enough the men would never let him live this down.

"You coming?" he asked her, and she shook her head.

A second before he dumped Jamie into the Jeep, she cheerfully announced, "Don't expect us back anytime soon."

14

THE SHORT RIDE BACK was silent, and Jamie wondered if Cole was too busy wallowing in regret. He'd shocked the living daylights out of her, and she was pretty sure Rachel and Jesse hadn't closed their mouths yet. Trace had laughed along with the other men who'd seen him pick her up like a sack of potatoes.

Barbara had been waiting at the window, and flung open the front door before Cole had the Jeep parked. Obviously the woman was anxious for news of the fire and her children, and Jamie had no business feeling disappointed that she and Cole couldn't have secretly slipped upstairs.

After issuing a quick assurance that she was fine, Jamie bounded up the stairs, leaving Cole behind to fill in details. She couldn't resist a backward glance when she got to the top, and found Cole's dark eyes watching her. His message was loud and clear, and she shuddered as she hurried to her room, losing all hope of sneaking in a shower before he came for her.

She'd just stripped off her soggy jeans and shirt when she heard the knock. Just in case she'd been overconfident in her assumption it was him, she pulled the door open slowly and peeked through the crack.

Cole's gaze drifted from her face to her semi-bare shoulder. "May I come in?"

She moved back, standing only in her bra and skimpy bikini panties, as he entered the room. "Did your mom see you?" she asked, immediately feeling like a dope.

He started unbuttoning his shirt.

"I can't believe you hauled me over your shoulder in front of everyone." She took a step backward, struggling to keep a lid on her excitement. Her pulse raced for an imaginary finish line, and her heart nearly flipped over in her chest. "Who said you could come in here and take off your clothes?"

His mouth twitched in amusement. "Seems to me you announced to all and sundry what you expected we'd be doing."

She thought back for a second. "Yeah, okay," she said, pushing her fingers through her wet hair and trying not to smile. "Whatever."

He unfastened the last button so that his shirt hung open.

Her breath caught. She already knew he had a mighty fine chest. Nice flat belly, a smattering of crisp black hair. How come she never noticed he wore his jeans so low? Or that wet denim could cling like that...? Holy crap.

The backs of her legs met the bed, and only then did she realize she'd been moving. In the nick of time she stopped herself from plopping down and getting the comforter wet.

Cole shrugged out of his shirt, then glanced around.

"Probably best to put it in the bathroom to dry," she murmured absently, more interested in that bulge behind his fly.

She forced her gaze up to the ridges of muscle spanning his taut belly, the contours of his chest. Then his face.

His eyes blazed as hot as the fire they'd fought. When he leisurely ran his heated gaze down her body, she made a small needy sound in the back of her throat she hoped he couldn't hear. It occurred to her that Cole was the kind of man that once he made up his mind there was no stopping him. Not that she had the slimmest intention of doing such a stupid thing. But the idea thrilled her.

"You gonna take off that bra and panties or shall I?" he asked calmly, appearing indifferent to the fact that he'd just caused an army of goose bumps to pop out on her skin.

She reached around to find the back clasp of her bra and unhooked it. The red silky cups loosened, and when she brought her arms to her sides, the straps slid off her shoulders.

Cole quickly tossed his drenched shirt through the bathroom door and unbuttoned his jeans. His eagerness made her laugh, until he pulled off her bra, his nostrils flaring as he bared her breasts.

Jamie struggled for her next breath. "We better grab a hot shower before the others come home," she said in a hoarse voice that didn't belong to her.

He lightly traced her aroused nipple, teased it with his thumb and forefinger. "Yeah, my hair smells like smoke."

"I thought that was mine."

"Shower," he murmured, touching the tip of his tongue to his lower lip, clearly unable to drag his gaze away from her breasts. "It's now or never."

"I want a shower." She pulled out of reach. "I *need* a shower."

"Now."

"Yes."

He went back to unbuttoning his jeans, and she headed for the bathroom because she knew if she stayed and watched, they'd end up on that bed.

She pushed aside the quaint daisy-patterned vinyl curtain and fiddled with the faucet, frustrated, trying too hard to get the right balance of hot and cold water. He came up behind her, slid a hand inside her panties and cupped her backside, his warm work-roughened palm stroking her sensitive skin.

"Why are these still on?" he whispered, his warm moist breath bathing her ear.

She groaned. "I can't get the temperature right."

He reached around her to take over, his long hard penis pressing against her ass and hip. She braced herself with one hand flattened to the tile wall and with her free one, tugged down her panties. He helped from behind, pulling the elastic past her thighs to her calves, while trailing light kisses down her spine.

Using her toes, she worked the panties to her ankles and then kicked them off. Cole slowly straightened, covering more territory with his enticing lips as he moved up to her neck. He'd abandoned the water faucet and used his hands and tongue and teeth to drive her crazy. Before she knew what was happening, he turned her around to face him and covered her mouth with his.

Their tongues met in a heated rush, and she clung to him, her fingers digging into the firm muscles of his shoulders. She could feel him, hard against her belly, taste his desire mixed with an odd desperation in his kiss. He skimmed his hands down her back, over the curve of her bottom, then cupped her cheeks, pulling her snugger still against his arousal.

As good as it felt, she couldn't wait. She forced a hand between their bodies and touched the silky swollen crown of his penis. He hissed in a breath, moved against her probing fingers.

"Check the water," he whispered, his voice a raspy flow of warm breath in her mouth.

Refusing to relinquish her newfound treasure, she stuck her other hand under the spray. "It's perfect."

He caught her by the waist, paused to look down at her firm grip of his erection. A ghost of a smile tugged at one side of his mouth. "Better let go or this is going to get tricky."

"Yeah." She laughed giddily, and glanced down at the raised lip of the old-fashioned shower. Falling on her ass while climbing into the stall was not her idea of romantic.

She let go and turned to gingerly step over the eight-inch

rim, then gained her footing on the wet floor. He followed her inside, and she grinned at how big he looked in the small space, his broad shoulders spanning to a matter of inches between the walls. They'd have little room to maneuver.

"What?" he asked, taking a nip at the side of her neck. "Anybody ever tell you not to look as if you're gonna laugh when a man gets naked?"

She reached for the soap. "With you in it, this shower looks like something from Barbie's dream house."

"This place was built in the 1800s, the upstairs addition around 1920." He took the soap from her and worked up a lather. "I can't recall when this room was last updated. We should've gone to mine. I have a nice big bathroom." His mouth curved in a sexy smile. "I could've done all manner of wicked things to you."

"Don't think you're off the hook...." She gasped when he slid his soapy hand between her thighs. "Okay," she said weakly. "I see we're on the same page."

He chuckled low in his throat, the husky sound sizzling over her skin like a light electrical charge. Everywhere he touched was ultra-sensitive—her legs, her arms, even her knees and elbows, for heaven's sake. And her breasts...oh, God, when he circled his slick palms around her nipples, she had to steady herself by shoving at the white tile wall on either side of her.

"Shampoo?" he asked, and then slid his tongue inside her mouth when she started to answer.

After a thorough sweep of her inner cheeks, her tongue, the roof of her mouth, he eased back, sucking in her lower lip between his as he retreated.

The shampoo was on the sink, which she thought she could reach from the shower if he gave her a single second. Not that she wanted him to stop. But then there was still the bed, queen-size, with lots of room to get creative.

"Shampoo," she muttered, and firmly twisted away from him, then swatted blindly at the daisy shower curtain.

It was a farther reach to the sink than she expected. She had to step one foot onto the bathmat and really stretch. She felt his teeth on her ass, and jerked, startled. "Not one to waste an advantage, are you?" she said with a shaky laugh, and snagged the bottle.

He licked his way up her spine and planted a kiss on her shoulder. "Nope," he said, then helped her squeeze back in to face him, the warm spray at her back feeling wonderful.

She wasn't sure what type of lover she'd imagined Cole to be. Although she hadn't given the matter much consideration, on some level she'd assumed he'd be laid-back, perhaps even more traditional in his approach. That was probably because he'd given her a hard time in the beginning, or maybe it was because his image as an upstanding, responsible member of the community seemed important to him. Whatever…this playful sexiness suited her just fine.

"Tilt your head back," he told her, squeezing shampoo into his scarred palm.

"You're going to wash my hair?" She'd never had a man do that before.

"That's the plan."

"It's already wet."

"I don't care about the spray. I don't want the sudsy water to get in your eyes." He caught her earlobe between his teeth and then nuzzled the side of her neck.

That was enough for her head to loll back and her eyes to drift closed. By the time his fingers began massaging her scalp, she was complete mush. How she managed to stay on her feet was astonishing—she ran her palms down his chest, smiling when she hit the mother lode. He was still rock-hard, and she wished she could see him. But feeling blindly was good, too.

Cole groaned, his hands stilling. "Jesus."

"What?" she asked, all innocence, and used the back of her wrist to wipe her closed eyes.

"Keep your head back." He closed his fist over her other probing hand. "And no touching."

"Why?"

"Because I'm gonna come, that's why," he growled, his voice low and gravelly.

"Oh. Got a hair trigger, have you?" Chuckling, she opened her eyes and blinked. Shampoo streamed in between her lids. She abruptly released him, squeezed her eyes shut again and used the heels of both hands to try to staunch the stinging. "Dammit."

He chuckled. "That's called frontier justice."

"Ha. Ha." She blindly felt for the towel hanging on the rack beyond the shower curtain. Suddenly it was in her hands, she was pretty sure with his help. "Dangerous talk for a guy who thinks he's going to get lucky tonight."

"I have insurance." He touched her breast, then toyed with her nipple before taking it into his mouth.

His ministration seemed to cure the stinging. She tossed the towel toward the sink and then threaded her fingers through his hair. He'd crouched in front of her, and rolled his tongue over her breast, around her aroused nipple, occasionally using his teeth and then soothing her again with the flat of his tongue. The wet she felt between her legs had nothing to do with the water raining down on them.

He couldn't be comfortable...they had to get out and dry off. Then again they hadn't finished, and if she were a nicer person she'd be shampooing his hair instead of nearly pulling it out at the roots. Except she wasn't breathing well or all that steady on her feet. He had a keen way of reducing her to a mindless, boneless lump.

Jamie used everything she had to pull herself together. She found the discarded shampoo bottle on the soap ledge, squirted the vanilla-scented cream into his hair. He ignored her. If you didn't include him dragging his mouth, all teeth and tongue and sharp sucks, down to her belly.

Quickly she worked up a lather, not easy when she had to fight the spraying water. She did a half-assed job, hoping she at least got rid of the smoke smell, and rinsed out the suds just as his mouth landed at the juncture of her thighs.

"No, up." She shoved at his shoulders.

He froze, his body tensing.

For a second, she didn't understand. And then she did. "No, no, it's not that I don't want you to do that. You look too uncomfortable scrunched up like that."

He leaned back, holding her hips, and gave her a crooked smile. Then he grimaced, squinting, when water dripped into his eyes.

"Poor baby." She tried not to laugh but he looked on the young side of twelve. "I know it stings," she said, fighting with the curtain then finding the towel she'd discarded. "We seriously have to get out of here before you end up a pretzel."

She turned off the water and gave him the towel. While he dried his face, she helped him up, impressed that he could still be so hard through all of that.

"Wait a minute," he said, blinking down at himself. "I didn't get all the soap off."

"I'll turn the water back on, but I'm getting out first."

"No." He reached for her arm but it was too slick.

"Yes," she said, laughing, slipping out of the stall. "Or we'll never get dry."

She pulled the curtain shut. Instead of drying off, she wiped the steam from the mirror over the sink. Just what she thought. Raccoon eyes. Really bad ones. Shit. She plucked tissues from the box behind the toilet seat and dabbed furiously.

The shower came to life briefly, then off. Cole ducked his head out. The vinyl curtain covered enough of him that he looked as if he were wearing a yellow daisy-print muumuu.

Jamie laughed, then covered her mouth when she heard

a noise. A floorboard creaked. She recognized it as coming from outside her bedroom door. Someone was out in the hall, either headed for his room or looking for them. Eyes wide, she silently pointed.

"So what?" Cole leaned over and lightly pinched her bottom. "Get me a towel."

"Shh. Your highness." She threw him the spare.

"It's probably Jesse. He's the only one with a room past ours." Cole blotted his face dry, and said, "What are you gonna do, tell my mother I didn't say, 'please pass the towel'?"

"Maybe. I know she raised you with better manners." She turned back to the mirror to finish repairing her face.

He came up behind her, pressing his erection against the cleft of her ass. "A gentleman…is that what you want, Jamie?"

"Screw you." Impossible to hide her smile as she turned to slide her arms around his neck.

He kissed her, slowly, gently, sending waves of pleasure through her body, yet making her impatient at the same time. She started to kiss him back in earnest, when he suddenly lifted his head. "Oh, hell."

"Um, not the reaction I'd hoped for."

"Condoms." He sighed. "They're in my room."

"Relax. I have a couple in my bag."

Surprise flickered in his eyes, and he gave an almost imperceptible shake of his head that somehow made her feel defensive for being a sensible, prepared woman. But then his sexy smile chased it away. "May not be enough."

"I am so telling your mother," she murmured against his curved mouth.

"Dare you."

Jamie laughed. "I wouldn't want to embarrass her."

"She has three boys."

"Ah, point taken. I'll still spare her."

"Right." He used his towel to dry her back, her butt and

the backs of her thighs, then tried to sneak in a detour that had her squirming and giggling.

"I hope this room is soundproof," she said, pushing away his hand and trying to stifle her silly girlish laughter.

"I reckon only Jesse can hear."

"Oh, God."

"I'm kidding." He finished drying himself off, his eyes tracking her as she did the same and then combed back her hair. "I need a trim," he said, slicking back his own dark locks. He caught his reflection in the mirror. Frowning, he rubbed his stubbly jaw. "I should've shaved first."

"I don't care."

His gaze fell to her throat, then moved to her breasts. "I don't want to hurt you."

"I'm tougher than I look."

"Think so?" He lightly bit her shoulder.

"Oh, honey, you better believe it."

The strangest expression flitted across his face. It almost looked like doubt. Why, because thunder rattled her? One small blip in her otherwise self-contained life. Jeez.

"Get the condoms. Please," he added, with an amused lift of his brow. Then touched her nipple, gently tugging at it. "I don't want to be interrupted again."

"Only because you said please." She could barely utter the few words without sounding as if she'd run a marathon.

She hurried to her bag, which she'd stuffed on the floor at the back of the closet, silently praying that she hadn't lied. Normally she kept a couple of condoms with her when she traveled, but with the excitement over Linda's wedding, it was possible Jamie had forgotten to pack them.

The notion stopped her. She'd barely thought about the gang. A week ago she'd been in a funk wondering what she'd do for the Labor Day long weekend, or whether she'd bother going alone to her neighbor's annual Halloween party. Good God, she hadn't even checked her messages in the past two days.

Or been online. This had to be a record.

Well, she sure as hell wouldn't check in now, or, she hoped, for the rest of the night.

"Something wrong?"

At the sound of Cole's voice, she turned and saw him standing outside the bathroom door, his lean nude body a sheer work of art. Just the right amount of sinew and crisp curling hair, and she wanted him, desperately, under her, on top of her, inside her.

She snapped out of her trance. "Wrong?" she repeated.

His face was dark, uncertain. "You look as if you're having second thoughts."

"What?" She realized she'd been just standing there, her hand on the closet knob. "No. The opposite. I was thinking that my friends must think I've dropped off the face of the earth."

"That's a good thing?" He moved to the bed and pulled down the quilt.

"You don't understand. I'm never without my phone." She dragged her bag out. "Or away from my website. I haven't given either one a thought."

"But you are now?"

"No. I… Don't try and figure out this convoluted brain of mine. It'll give you a headache." She found the small pink case and the two condoms inside.

He was right there, pulling her to her feet, running his hands over her body. "I can't believe how much I want you," he murmured into her hair, and then picked her up.

She squealed like a little girl. "If you end up throwing out your back, I'm going to be so pissed."

He laid her on the bed. "I'm touched by your concern."

"Come here." She didn't have to tell him.

Cole followed her down, half his body covering hers as he kissed her chin, then her lips and kneaded her breast. He smelled of rain, warm flesh and her vanilla shampoo. She forgot how to breathe when he deepened the kiss, his tongue mating with hers, his erection lying hot and heavy across her belly.

15

COLE WOULDN'T BE ABLE to hold out for long. Twice in the shower he'd been so close to coming it shocked him. Hell, he'd been seventeen the last time he had to recite multiplication tables in his head to keep from making a jackass out of himself. Good to know he still remembered his lessons, he thought wryly.

He slid his hand between her thighs, and prodded her eager legs apart. Skin soft and smooth like silk everywhere he touched. But feeling her wasn't enough. He wanted to look at her, all of her, taste her, but that would put him in the danger zone again.

"We don't have to wait," she whispered, as though reading his mind. "We do have two condoms."

Groaning, he lowered his mouth to her breast, suckled her nipple until she groaned with him. Moving his hand higher inside her thigh, his fingers brushed the damp curls that threatened his restraint. She shifted impatiently. That's all the urging he needed to find her clit, find the slick heat that let him easily slide his finger inside her.

He went deep, and she gasped, clenching her muscles around him. His cock jumped. Dammit, he had to sheath himself. Now. "Where did you—"

She reached behind her and felt around the bedside table, quickly locating the silver packet and tearing it open. They both had to shift positions, and it killed him to have to pull his finger out of her but she was suddenly in charge. He'd put out his hand for the condom, but she ignored him.

Instead, she shimmied down his body until she was mouth-level with his cock. "Jamie, no." Not that he didn't want that, but he'd come in seconds.

She just smiled and briefly kissed the engorged crown, then leaned back and rolled on the condom. Moisture from his cock glistened on her lower lip, and he was back to multiplying. Except, damned if he knew what two-times-eight equaled. Or what his name was.

"Now, where were we?" She crawled back up to him, skimming his belly with her breasts, taunting him with those sweet hard nipples.

"Sit on top of me." He gripped her hips, gently urging her to straddle him, not afraid to beg if he had to. "I want to look at you."

Obliging him, she swung a leg over his thighs, and God help him but he couldn't stop staring, even though the glimpse she'd allowed him was all too swift. With her pubic hair shaved and trimmed all nice and tidy, the view had been enough to stop a man's heart.

Her lean compact body was such a nice fit for him that all he had to do was raise his arms and close his hands over her high firm breasts. Jamie made that soft sighing sound, laced with enough of a whimper that it pushed him further to the edge, and he hadn't even entered her yet.

She lifted herself over his cock, toyed with him for a few moments, and then slid down on him in agonizing slowness. She moved a little, small settling movements as if adjusting to the invasion of her body, and driving him so friggin' nuts he clenched his jaw and slammed his head back against the pillow.

When she leaned over to kiss him, she forced his cock to an angle that nearly finished him.

"This is going to be fast," he warned.

"As long as you don't fall asleep on me right after." She sucked his lower lip into her mouth, fisted his hair and rocked back and forth, her aroused pink nipples creating an unbearable friction on his chest.

"Christ, Jamie."

"Hmm?"

His low guttural moan seemed to shake the room. He curled up slightly, slipped a hand behind her nape, holding her still and kissing her hard until they were both panting. She moved back into a sitting position, taking him with her, clenching her muscles around his cock so tightly, his last shred of control snapped.

JAMIE WATCHED COLE'S EYES close and his strong, sweat-slick body begin to tremble. When his groan grew so loud someone was bound to hear, she clamped a hand over his mouth, then replaced it with her own mouth.

He quieted some, reached around and squeezed her ass, pulling her against him as he thrust up inside her...harder, deeper...until she was hot and cold and close to shattering. Never had she been filled so completely before. It was both scary and wonderful, and as much as she was trying not to come yet, if he kept sucking on her tongue...thrusting into her...

Before she knew it, his thumb found her clit. She gasped and tried to evade his hand. She'd never been one to have multiple orgasms, and God, but she didn't want it to end so soon. But he was too strong, too determined. No amount of effort on her part could get him to stop, and the pressure kept building until she couldn't take it anymore.

Her body tensed, her climax swelled, the sensation so intense she had to press her lips together to keep from crying out as she convulsed so violently that she fell forward, and Cole wrapped his arms around her trembling body, hugging her tight, kissing her hair as spasm after spasm overtook her.

Long after the last sensual waved crashed over her, Jamie lay on top of his heaving chest. He stroked her back and pressed soft kisses to her temple. When she made a move to roll off him, he held her firmly and whispered words she wasn't coherent enough yet to understand.

Vaguely she was aware that the storm outside seemed to have reawakened. Thunder clapped in the distance. The sound didn't faze her. Encircled by Cole's strong arms, feeling the steady beat of his heart, she felt safe and warm. Content to stay where she was, she buried her face in his neck, inhaling his musky masculine scent.

After their breathing evened out, and reality began to seep in, she blearily eyed the bedside clock. He was supposed to be outside keeping watch. "Are you going back out?"

"I can't move."

"You want me off?" She tried to push herself up.

"No." He tightened his hold. "Stay," he said in a raw, husky voice. "Right here."

She lifted her head and smiled at him. "I'm too heavy."

He kissed the tip of her nose. "You're just right."

"Cole?"

"Hmm?" His lips were now on hers, lightly brushing, nibbling, coaxing.

"I can't breathe."

He stopped, and loosened his arms around her. Then he started laughing, the rumbling in his chest teasing her breasts. "Better?"

She inhaled deeply. "Being smothered did have its upside."

Without warning, he rolled over, taking her with him until she was pinned to the mattress. He was careful not to crush her, using his elbows to leverage himself while he gazed down at her.

"I don't think Rachel would take kindly to me smothering one of her guests," he said.

She flinched. Stupid, because she knew he hadn't meant anything by the remark. He was just trying to be funny.

"What's wrong?" He stared deep into her eyes.

"I'm a little drowsy. Aren't you?"

"Nope." He nibbled at her chin, then ran the tip of his tongue to her ear.

It tickled, and she squirmed, felt him getting hard again. "You're kidding."

"About?" He moved down to her breasts, flicking his tongue over her nipple, eliciting an immediate response.

When he wedged a hand between her thighs, she realized he wasn't kidding at all.

"THE MOUNTAINS ARE BEAUTIFUL this morning. They look greener than usual," Jamie said to Rachel, while lingering over her third cup of coffee and trying not to yawn.

Jamie had slept late and missed breakfast with the other guests who'd blessedly left on their preplanned excursions. Rachel had saved her a blueberry muffin and cubed cantaloupe, but all Jamie wanted was another gallon of strong coffee.

"That seems to happen right after a heavy rain. I don't know why." Rachel had finished clearing the dishes, and brought a cup of coffee with her to join Jamie at the dining room table. "You don't look as though you slept well. After the night you had, I figured you'd crash hard."

Jamie coughed, gained control of herself, then stared at Rachel, grateful that she hadn't choked. Sure, Rachel had seen Cole carry Jamie to the truck and probably guessed something might have happened, but to make a remark like that...

Rachel hid behind her cup, but not before Jamie saw a grin blossoming on her friend's face.

Oh, crap.

Embarrassment stung Jamie's cheeks, made her wish she was sitting under the table instead of across from Rachel. She was talking about putting out the fire, not what had happened with Cole and Jamie in her room.

Jamie cleared her throat. "Yeah, I was pretty tired."

Rachel pressed her lips together. "Me, too. I almost bailed on Hilda this morning."

Jamie glanced around the room. "So…"

After an awkward silence, Rachel burst out laughing. "Just remember, I'm not the one who brought it up."

"I have no idea what you're talking about. That's my story, and I'm sticking to it."

"I'm sorry, it's just…you don't know my brother. Well, yeah, obviously you do, but what he did last night by picking you up…" Rachel dabbed at her watery eyes. "Let's just say every jaw hit the ground. Dutchy and the boys will be talking about last night forever."

"Great." Jamie sighed. "Cole will love that." It probably meant he'd be staying clear of her for the next three days. As it was he'd left her room early, though she'd reasoned that he normally had his coffee and was out of the house by sunup. Still…

"That's the beauty of it. For once in his adult life, my brother acted on impulse and didn't give a rat's ass about anything else."

"God forbid I'm the one who ends up sullying his reputation."

Rachel grinned. "It's not like that. It's not even that he cares what people think." She shrugged. "He just never does anything that's gossip worthy."

"What about you?" Jamie asked, anxious to change the subject. "I bet you and Trace have set quite a few tongues wagging."

Rachel's expression changed in an instant. Her pensive gaze drifted toward the window, and then she smiled a little.

"Trace hasn't made headlines in ages. As a kid he was such a troublemaker, nothing he does shocks anyone." Her eyes came back to Jamie. "People did love talking about me and Matt Gunderson. Then he left, two years later I went off to school and the town found someone else to talk about. More coffee?"

Jamie was dying to hear more but all she said was, "I'll get it. How about you?"

Rachel was up in a flash. "Stay put. I'll fill a carafe for us."

Jamie drained her cup and thought about Cole as she waited for Rachel to return. If someone asked her to describe last night with him, she couldn't do it. She'd written what seemed like a gazillion travel blogs in the past seven years, quirky ones, serious ones, balancing information with entertainment. They usually wrote themselves quickly, effortlessly; jeez, she could practically write them in her sleep.

But when thinking about last night? There were no words. *Perfect* was all that came to mind. Cole and *perfect*. The man didn't even seem as if he could be for real. Hot, sexy, thoughtful, a body that wouldn't quit, and those hands… The man had skills.…

Remembering the sexy things he'd whispered in her ear when she'd come the second time, she felt her cheeks get warm. She'd never expected Cole to be a talker.… He'd shocked her, but in a really good way.

Rachel appeared armed with coffee and a basket of muffins. "Fresh out of the oven," she said, setting down the plate, eyeing the one Jamie had left untouched. "Hilda insisted I feed you."

Jamie sighed. "I love Hilda. I need a Hilda in my life. I'm so sick of takeout food."

"Ah, call me crazy but you could cook for yourself," Rachel suggested.

"Um, there's a scary thought." Jamie shuddered. "Ever hear of Rita Rudner?"

"The comedienne?"

Jamie nodded. "I like her take on cooking. She says a recipe is like reading a science-fiction novel. She gets to the end and thinks, 'that'll never happen.'"

Rachel laughed.

Nodding sagely, Jamie picked up her muffin. "Rita knows what she's talking about."

Someone had let the back door slam, and Rachel turned her head to look toward the kitchen. "Gotta be Trace. Hilda's smacking him upside the head about now."

Cole walked into the dining room, yanking the black Stetson off his head, and Jamie's heart about somersaulted out of her chest.

With raised brows, Rachel watched him approach the table. "Mom sees you walking with those boots on this floor and you're dead."

"You gonna tattle, pip-squeak?" He winked at Jamie, and snatched one of the muffins.

"Someone's in an awfully good mood. Wonder why?"

Jamie glared in warning at Rachel, who looked far too pleased with herself. Let her rile her brother another time. Yes, he was in a damn fine mood, and Jamie wanted to keep it that way.

"You just start breakfast?" he asked Jamie, after glancing at the muffin she still held in midair.

She put it down. "Sort of…yeah."

"Want to go for a ride with me? We can take some muffins with us."

"Sure."

Rachel snorted. "You'd rather go riding with him than sit here with me?"

Before Jamie could give her a snarky answer, Cole said, "Make yourself useful, pip-squeak, and fix us a thermos of coffee."

Rachel gave him a one-finger salute that made Jamie grin.

Cole shook his head in mock disgust. "All that tuition and that's what you learned."

"Actually," Rachel said sweetly as she got up from the table, "I learned that for free from you and Jesse."

A guilty smile twitched at the corners of Cole's mouth. "You have me mixed up with Trace."

"Good to know he's a lousy liar, huh?" Rachel said to Jamie as she picked up the basket of muffins and the carafe. On her way to the kitchen she gave her brother a long look. "Wow, you are in a good mood. It's almost annoying."

He popped another piece of muffin into his mouth and chewed, looking faintly amused with Rachel. As soon as she left, Cole came around the table, his gaze steady on Jamie.

Her erratically speeding pulse nearly jumped the track when he bent over and kissed her mouth. The kiss was brief but so unexpected that for a moment she stopped breathing.

"Mornin'," he whispered.

"Morning back at you."

"Do you remember me leaving?"

"Of course." She sounded calm and cool, when all she wanted to do was wrap her arms and legs around him. Drag him down to the floor and replay everything they did last night.

"You were pretty groggy." He lowered himself into the chair next to hers, angling his long lean legs so that they grazed her calves under the table.

"Did I say something weird?"

"Nope," he said, touching her cheek, one side of his mouth hiking up in amusement. "Just begged me to—" Abruptly he stopped, withdrew his hand and glanced toward the parlor.

Out of the corner of her eye, she saw his mother coming from that direction. "To what?" Jamie taunted softly, holding his dare-you gaze for several seconds before turning to give Barbara a smile. "Hi."

"Good morning, Jamie. Heard you had quite a night."

In spite of herself, Jamie blushed like a virginal bride. Under the table, Cole bumped her knee with his leg. She couldn't decide if she should ignore him or glare. "I have a feeling I was more a hindrance than a help."

"Not from what I heard." Barbara's warm smile reached her eyes, and then she ran a speculative gaze over Cole. "What are you doing here this time of day?"

"I'm taking Jamie for a ride to Elk Valley."

"Oh." Barbara blinked. "Well, good."

"If Rachel will hurry up with our coffee and muffins," he called loudly over his shoulder in the direction of the kitchen.

Sighing, as only a mother who'd refereed her share of childhood battles could, Barbara checked her watch. "As much as I'd love to stay for the fireworks, I've got to run. Need anything from town?"

"No, thanks." Cole glanced at Jamie.

So did Barbara. "And you?"

Her reaction to the simple meaningless gesture took Jamie by surprise. Confusing emotions surged through her and welled up in her chest. To them the other women were clearly paying guests. Jamie they consistently treated as if she were one of the family. In big ways and tiny ways she shouldn't even acknowledge, she'd been drawn into the fold, and it touched her, big-time. God, she must be hormonal.

Jamie cleared her throat. "No, thank you. I'm good."

"Can I save you a trip into town?" Cole asked his mom. "I've got to run in for a haircut and to pick up some lumber later. Figured I'd take Jamie for a late lunch, if she wants," he said, turning to Jamie.

She just nodded, and looked to Barbara for her reaction.

Apparently she didn't find it odd that her son wanted to take Jamie out for a meal. "Thanks, honey, but I'm meeting Thelma and Liz." Barbara started up the stairs, and without looking back, added, "If you wear your work boots in here again, I will tan your hide."

Grimacing and grinning at the same time, Cole rubbed the back of his neck. To Jamie he mouthed, "Eyes in the back of her head."

"Told ya." Rachel, who'd obviously overheard, came from the kitchen with a wide grin. "Here." She passed Jamie the thermos and a brown paper sack. "Dole out the muffins as you see fit."

Feigning annoyance, Cole picked his hat up off the table and settled the Stetson on his head. "In the end, you women always stick together."

Jamie groaned. "You did not just say that."

Rachel gave him a haughty look and tossed her long auburn hair. "It's more like—cream always rises to the top."

"Come on. We're outta here." Cole slid an arm around Jamie's shoulders and ushered her toward the front door.

His arm fell away as they walked toward the stables, mostly because it was hot and awkward maneuvering on uneven ground, and clearly not because he was tense. Her heart did a little happy dance.

The whole morning had seemed surreal. From the moment he'd left her room, she'd expected the worst. That he'd avoid her like crazy, and stay away from the house from sunup until dark.

But no, he was taking her riding.

"What are you smiling about?" he asked, stopping in front of Ginger's stall.

"It's a beautiful day. Why not?" She patted the chestnut's nose and turned to Cole. "See, you're smiling, too."

"I am. I'm taking a gorgeous woman with me to one of the prettiest places on earth. We might even sit awhile. Watch the eagles. I mean, a man can't be on duty 24/7, right?" With a finger, he pushed back the brim of his hat and lowered his mouth to hers.

She wasn't sure if it was his eager kiss that had her trembling down to her toes, or the fact that he'd actually listened to her. And that he'd thought what she had to say had merit. It took a rare kind of man to admit such a thing. But then she'd already known he was ten kinds of special.

He hauled her body against him, his arousal pressed to her belly, his fingers digging into her bottom. That he was already so hard made her wonder where his mind had been from the house to the stable.

"I want you right now," he whispered, his low husky voice an intimate murmur in the dim cavernous building.

A laugh bubbled up in the back of her throat. "Here?"

"Yeah, here." He nuzzled her neck, and she could feel his smile. "Problem?"

"Um…"

His gravelly chuckle made her tingle. "We'll wait. But not long."

16

THAT EVENING, ALONE in her room, Jamie lay back against the pillows she'd double-stacked and closed her eyes, wondering if she had time for a quick nap. Twenty minutes tops and she'd be good, ready for anything. She shivered with delight, because with Cole anything really meant *anything*.

The man was creative and insatiable, and certainly not shy about where he spread a blanket. Their morning horseback ride had ended at a shady green spring not far from the ranch. He'd been concerned about her being sore from getting back in the saddle too soon, while she'd been more worried about someone discovering them frolicking in the raw, her riding him. Hells bells, wouldn't that have been the icing on the cake?

Morning had stretched to afternoon, and they hadn't made it to town because he'd gotten a call that he was needed in the north pasture, but all in all it was a ridiculously excellent day.

Soon to be resumed after Cole finished payroll. She glanced at the bedside clock. Even if she did sleep longer than twenty minutes, he'd come in and wake her. She only wished he'd lie down, sleep, no monkey business. He had to be dead-tired after the fire, then last night and working most of the day. Even his dinner had been eaten on the fly because of an emergency phone call. But knowing him, he'd consider sleep a waste of time.

Jamie smiled at the ceiling. Maybe if she thoroughly and utterly exhausted him...

She heard a soft knock and pushed up to a sitting position. Too soon. Couldn't be Cole. Maybe Rachel. "Come in."

The door opened. It was him, in his ubiquitous jeans, though these weren't so faded, no Western-cut work shirt. Instead he wore only a black T-shirt that snugly fit his lean body, and his hair was damp and slicked back.

"What happened? You can't be finished with payroll that fast."

He closed the door behind him. "Jesse's doing it for me."

"Oh."

"You disappointed I'm early?"

"No. It's just...why does Jesse think you can't do it?"

A roguish smile curved Cole's mouth as he stretched out beside her, sliding his hand under her top. "I told him I had too many wicked things I wanted to do to you and we'd end up with no sleep."

"You did not." She studied his face, not sure what sort of secrets brothers exchanged. Well, hell, she told Linda, Kaylee and Jill a lot.

"No, I did not." He pushed her top up and planted a kiss on her belly. "I'm sure he figured it out by himself. And that's why he offered."

"Oh, my God. Talk about a family affair. Rachel definitely knows, so does Jesse. Your mom suspects something. That leaves only Trace in the dark."

Cole chuckled. "Trace knew the moment I picked you up and threw you in Jesse's Jeep."

"Oh, right, how could I forget? Everyone on the whole damn ranch knows our business."

He lifted his head, his expression contrite. "I didn't think of it quite that way." He pulled her shirt back down. "I'm sorry, Jamie. But it's not as if they know anything concrete. Dutchy and the boys probably think you told me to take a hike."

"Now why would they think that?" She held his face in her hands and smiled.

"Because you're gorgeous and can have anyone you want. Why settle for a burned-out backwater old cowboy like me?"

She laughed, then kissed him hard. "I believe you're fishing for a compliment, Cole McAllister."

His serious brown eyes told her otherwise. He lowered his gaze to her mouth, and traced her lips with the roughened pad of his thumb. "You're so soft."

"Just so we're clear, I don't care who knows. But I figured you might. You're the one who lives here."

His thumb stilled, just for a second, and then he drew it down to her chin. "I heard from Noah today. Sheriff Calder. They found Mrs. Clements's four-wheeler. It went missing the day you arrived."

"I remember." She came up onto her elbows. "What about your trailer?"

"No news unfortunately, but Roker's missing flatbed wound up in a field about ten miles from his place. And the four-wheeler wasn't even a theft. Separate issue from the Sundance. Technically, yeah, it was stolen, but the guy who took it used to work for Mrs. Clements. They had a dispute, nothing new with her—she's got a sharp tongue and a temper to go with it—but she refused to pay Toby for two weeks' work, so the kid took the four-wheeler as payment." Cole shrugged. "Toby is young and it was wrong, but he's got a wife and two kids of his own to feed, and Clements can be completely unreasonable. Hard to feel sorry for her."

"So does this Toby guy have to go to jail?"

"He's there now."

"Can't anyone talk to the woman, convince her not to press charges?"

Cole smiled and brushed back her hair. "If I knew you were gonna get this riled, I wouldn't have told you."

"I'm not riled…. What about his wife and kids?"

"They'll be okay. No one around here will let them go hungry. Everything will work out."

She settled back against the pillows and tried to relax. "I'm glad you told me. It's not as if I can do anything about it, just that…" She liked that he talked to her not as a prelude to sex, but because he assumed she might be interested in what happened around Blackfoot Falls. Surprisingly, she was.

"What?"

"I wish you had news about your trailer. And I'm sorry, maybe I'm not catching on, but that flatbed trailer, that has to be connected, right?" She skimmed a palm over his bulging right biceps, where his close-fitting sleeve met skin. He flexed the muscle, and she smiled.

"I don't know." He shook his head as he exhaled a heavy breath. "It's just damn strange."

"So basically you're back to square one."

"'Fraid so."

"That means Gunderson is still a suspect."

"Gotta be careful there. No evidence."

"Guess none of us liking him doesn't count, huh?"

Cole grinned. "I'll tell Noah you weighed in," he said, and kissed the tip of her nose.

She picked up the hand that lay idle on her belly and kissed his scarred palm. "I'm sorry this happened to you."

He pulled away, and she instantly regretted bringing up the subject. Then relaxed when she saw him yank off his shirt and toss it aside. "It was a long time ago." He started unbuttoning her blouse. "Water under the bridge, as they say." He finished and unfastened the front clasp of her bra. "I'm sorry you're afraid of thunder, and what you went through to cause the fear."

She sat up, and he pushed the blouse off one shoulder and

then the other. "Guess we both had a bite taken out of our childhood," she said, breathless. He'd pushed the bra cups aside and bared her breasts.

Cole urged her to lie down again, and laved one of her nipples with his skilled tongue. She unsnapped his jeans and drew down the zipper very slowly because he was already hard, his arousal straining his fly. A moment later she felt his hand on her own jeans, and in no time he'd stripped her down to her pink lace panties.

Without realizing it, she'd been clutching his arm, her nails digging into his skin. She took a deep steadying breath and loosened her hold. His gaze locked on hers, he shoved his jeans down his hips, sat back and then quickly rid himself of every stitch. She didn't try to help, didn't even offer, simply soaked in the pleasure of watching his rippling chest muscles. Relished the knowledge that his impressive erection was all for her.

"You seem awfully pleased with yourself," he said, with the beginning of a smile on his lips.

"I do have you right where I want you."

"Funny, I was thinking the same thing." He slid his hands down her body, catching the elastic of her panties with two fingers and slipping the delicate lace down her thighs, her calves. Then they were gone.

He picked up her right foot and kissed the inside of her ankle, then reversed his path up her leg, continuing to press warm moist kisses against her sensitive skin. When he got to the softer, fleshier part of her thigh, she sucked in a breath and instinctively tensed.

"Relax, Jamie," he murmured, switching from his lips to using his tongue.

He spread her legs wider and his mouth found her with a deftness that had her arching off the bed and clutching his hair. As he explored her with his tongue, his hands sneaked beneath her so he had complete control over her hips. Jamie had to bite her own wrist to keep her cries from waking the whole house as he pulled her into a full-body orgasm.

Which was just the beginning. He entered her while she was still trembling and trying to breathe without gasping. She'd been so caught up in her own pleasure she hadn't even noticed him climbing up the bed, settling between her thighs. But when he thrust into her so hard she slid up the bed, he got her complete attention.

Jesus, the way he looked at her as he curved over her body. As if he was shutting out the rest of the world, staking his claim.

With any other man, she probably would have made a move of her own, asserted her independence and dared him to try again, but not with Cole. Not with his hot breath on her cheek, the wild look in his eyes.

All she could do, wanted to do, was wrap her legs around his slim hips, slip her hand around the nape of his neck and pull him down into a kiss that tasted like sex and need and promises.

When he came, he held her so tightly she could barely breathe.

"You realize everyone is going to want to know who you are," Cole said the next day as they drove toward Blackfoot Falls.

"They'll figure out I'm a guest at the Sundance." Jamie inched closer and laid a hand on Cole's thigh. "Besides, I already met Marge and some other lady. Forgot her name."

He kept his gaze on the road, but smiled and slid his arm around her shoulders, urging her closer. "You'll still get a bunch of questions."

Jamie laughed.

"You think I'm kidding?"

"No, it's not that." She sighed and snuggled closer. "If someone told me I'd be riding in a big old black pickup truck, sitting in the middle of a bench seat next to a tall hunky cowboy, his arm around me like we were teenagers out of a fifties movie, I would've asked if they were high."

Cole pulled back and gave her a long serious look.

She blinked. God, that had sounded awful. "Not that there's anything wrong with a pickup, or cowboys...."

Amusement gleamed in his eyes. "You think I'm hunky?"

She squeezed his thigh hard, which made little impact—too much muscle. "Just for that, if anyone asks I'm telling them I'm a hooker you picked up at a Billings truck stop."

Cole snorted. "Oh, that would be grist for the rumor mill, all right."

"We could make a bet on how long it takes for the story to get back to your mom."

"Let's not."

Jamie mimicked a clucking chicken, and Cole pulled the truck off to the side of the two-lane road.

She glanced behind to see if anyone was coming. "What are you doing?"

"I thought you wanted to play hooker and the trucker." He caught her wrist and kissed her palm. He slid his other hand inside her blouse.

She fought him, laughing and sputtering. "Stop. We're only a few miles from town...and there's a car coming...."

"Who's the chicken now?"

She shoved him away and tugged down her blouse, still giggling. "Okay, you win."

"Yeah? What do I win?"

"What do you want?"

The teasing glint left his eyes. He lifted a lock of her hair and rubbed the strands between his fingers. "Don't go to Sadie's tomorrow night."

"Sadie's?" Jamie frowned. "Oh, right...Sadie's." She slumped back. "Oh, my God, tomorrow is Friday already." How was it possible? She was scheduled to leave on Saturday. "Wow, where did the week go? I haven't even opened my laptop in days."

He smiled. "Is that so bad?"

"Yeah, when that's how I make my living."

His smile faded, and after checking the side mirror, he got them back on the road. "What are you doing over there? Come sit next to this cowboy."

"Only if you'll whisper sweet nothings in my ear." She scooted her butt closer, relieved that the mood hadn't gone south. Something had shifted though, only for a few moments, but it was there.

"Depends."

"On?"

"If you're going to Sadie's or not."

"Oh…" She thought about torturing him for a few more minutes. It would be only fair, considering his use of extortion. But she didn't feel like teasing him. She wished she hadn't remembered she was leaving in two days. "Not. I'm pretty sure Rachel will forgive me. With tomorrow being my last night here and all."

She held her breath, waiting for his response…waiting for him to ask her to stay longer, express disappointment…anything that showed he cared. She knew he did. He'd shown her in many small ways.

But how much did he care?

His hand had tightened on the wheel, his arm around her shoulders tensed. "Your last night, huh?" he said quietly.

"I booked my stay for a week."

"I reckon you have another trip planned right after this."

"Not really. I have three more scheduled this year, but not until next month and the end of October." She waited, hoping he'd ask her to stay. She could do it, no sweat, even for an extra week. Though she had to be careful and spend more time chatting on her website.

The truth was, she wasn't ready to leave, but he had to ask. This wasn't up to her alone, not anymore.

Someone behind them honked.

Cole ducked his head, glanced in the rearview mirror and lifted the hand he'd left dangling off her shoulder to wave at the driver. His nonchalance in returning his arm around her, then giving her a light squeeze, gave her hope.

"Any chance you can stay a few days longer?" The question was as casual as the wave, and her enthusiasm waned a bit.

"I could."

Silence, and then, "But?"

She turned and studied his profile. He carefully kept his gaze trained on the road, almost as if he didn't want to meet her eyes. "I don't know if Rachel has an opening. She might have booked my room."

He looked at her then, his brows furrowing. "I didn't mean stay as a paid guest. You'd stay with me in my room."

Her entire nervous system jumped into overdrive. "Wouldn't that be kind of weird?" she asked, her mind already racing ahead, trying to analyze what this meant.

"With the family?" His eyes back on the road, he shrugged. "I've never had a woman spend the night before, and it might be uncomfortable at first…" The way his voice trailed off, she suspected he regretted his offer. "Hell, we're both adults, and it's not as if everyone doesn't like you. But if you think it's too awkward, we'll make sure you have your own room."

This was what she wanted. Yes, he'd tiptoed around the topic a bit, but he wanted her to stay. "I'll check online later, make a couple of calls," she said, her gaze on the town looming ahead. "I have to quit fooling around and update my blog, but I'm sure I can swing another week."

"Yeah?"

"Yeah."

At his slow sexy smile, heat surged through her body. If

they hadn't been approaching town, she would've told him to pull over so she could give him a preview of what awaited him tonight. She slid her hand over his thigh, rubbed her palm across his fly. Was the man ever not hard?

But already another truck had pulled alongside them, the driver honking his horn, the passenger grinning and waving as if he hadn't seen Cole in years.

Cole lifted his hand in perfunctory acknowledgment, and muttered, "Don't you just love small towns."

COLE STEPPED OUT OF the barber shop onto the sidewalk and rubbed the back of his clean-shaven neck. He'd let Sherman hack off a good two inches when he'd asked for a trim and already Cole regretted the shorter cut. Should've waited. Jamie claimed she liked his hair the way it was.

He had to laugh at himself. Since when did he care about what a woman thought of his hair? 'Course, she'd had one hand wrapped around his cock when she'd shared her opinion last night. He suspected that had a lot to do with his reaction.

Shading his eyes, he squinted toward Abe's Variety. They were supposed to meet there, then go to Marge's for lunch. Hell, he didn't have time for any of this cavorting but it wasn't as though he took much time off. Hadn't even played poker with the boys in months.

Leaving his hat off his damp hair, he headed toward Abe's, where he'd left the truck. If Jamie wasn't there yet, she'd show up soon enough. Not much to see or do in Blackfoot Falls. He walked past the bank and the *Salinas Gazette* office, which had its lights out. The weekly newspaper had come out yesterday, so Fred, the owner, editor and sole employee, was likely spending the day sipping beer and whiskey in Sadie's Watering Hole next door.

Cole had no sooner stepped off the sidewalk to cross Main when Wallace Gunderson and Avery Phelps wobbled out of the bar, both of them in high spirits considering half the time

Avery hated Gunderson's guts. Cole figured today Gunderson was buying so all was temporarily forgiven.

Having nothing to say to either of them, he picked up his pace.

"McAllister!" It was Gunderson. "What's your hurry, son?"

Son. Out of the bastard's mouth, the word grated on every one of Cole's nerves. But no need for a scene, or for him to get heated, so he waited for the two men to catch up. He'd be polite, see what they wanted, then be on his way. If Gunderson was shit-faced enough, maybe he'd say something that would help Noah nail him on the theft.

Avery took the lead, his distinctive bow-legged gait making him look as if he'd been born on a horse. Before he reached Cole, he said, "Heard you had some trouble out at your place."

"The fire?" Cole knew damn well the man meant the trailer theft. He shrugged. "Lightning strike. No damage to speak of."

"Hadn't heard about that." Avery frowned. "I was referring to the theft of your trailer."

Red in the face and panting slightly, Gunderson joined them. His breath was strong enough to crack a mirror, but he didn't seem particularly drunk. "Pretty low, stealin' a man's trailer, no matter how empty your belly." His apparent sincerity gave Cole pause. "I'm keeping everything locked these days." Gunderson's mouth twisted in a nasty smirk. "If it had to happen, can't say I'm sorry it was to you."

Yeah, that sounded more like the bastard. "Much as I hate to break this up, I'm meeting someone." Cole gave them a cool smile and a slight nod. "Gentlemen."

"You know when this thieving business all started, don't ya?" Avery called after him. "Right after you turned your daddy's fine ranch into a fancy boarding house." He cursed. "Dude ranch, my bony ass."

Cole ignored him, kept walking, even when Avery kept

spouting more bullshit. No sense in Cole getting his back up and ruining his day with Jamie. He was going to have words with Gunderson and Avery, plenty of them. Later. After Jamie left.

Shit. The thought didn't improve his sinking mood. He didn't want her to go. Hell, he knew she had to leave eventually. He'd known from the get-go, but he'd never expected to become this attached to her. She was nothing like other city women he'd met. He'd crossed paths with enough of them, Rachel's college friends, tourists when he'd gone to Billings or Great Falls for livestock auctions.

Jamie was different. She was laid-back, funny. How he'd ever thought she wasn't the single prettiest woman he'd ever seen was a mystery. Damn. It didn't hurt that she was smart as a whip, passionate, too. Jamie had a good heart. Yeah, maybe he was biased. He smiled thinking about her, his mood back on the upswing.

Ruth Wilson came out of the Clip and Curl patting her poufy new hairdo and returned the smile she thought had been meant for her. She'd been his seventh-grade teacher and would've gotten one anyway. He added a comment about the hot weather, and then entered Abe's Variety.

He didn't see Jamie, but Louise and Sadie were standing near the register gabbing with Abe as if they had nothing to do, and mostly they didn't. They all looked over at him.

"Figured we'd see you today," Louise said.

He knew the remark had something to do with Jamie, but he'd humor them. "Why's that?"

"Your friend's back in town." Louise beamed, clearly delighted that she was first with the news, while behind her Abe rolled his eyes toward the ceiling.

"I know." Cole picked up a dusty pack of breath mints and tossed them onto the counter to be rung up. "I drove her in."

Sadie blinked. "Didn't she say she just got off the bus?"

Louise frowned. "That's what I heard."

"Ask her yourself," Abe said, and motioned with his chin at the same time the bell over the door jingled.

Cole turned.

Bella entered, saw him, lit up like a star on top of a Christmas tree. Hurrying the rest of the way, she threw her arms around his neck. "Hello, sugar. Boy, have I missed you."

On impact, Cole stumbled back, his arms automatically going around her to steady them.

Then he saw Jamie standing in the doorway.

17

"AREN'T YOU A SIGHT for sore eyes?" The blonde leaned back to look at Cole. Bubbling over with laughter, she hugged him again. "I swear you get better looking every time I come home. Doesn't he just keep getting cuter, Sadie?"

The heavyset fifty-something brunette snorted in agreement, her amused gaze brimming with curiosity as it settled on Jamie. In fact, Abe, the store's owner, and the other woman Jamie had met a few days ago were all staring at her.

So was Cole, looking as if he'd swallowed a whole pan of Hilda's corn bread. He transferred his attention to the other woman, politely extricating himself from her enthusiastic hug. "Bella, I didn't know you were coming home."

"Nobody did." She shrugged her slim shoulders. "Me included. I got tired of auditioning for stupid shampoo commercials and decided I needed me some fresh air and a few helpings of good ol' Cole McAllister." At his apprehensive expression, she laughed and lightly hit his chest. "Just teasing, sugar. But I do expect you to buy me supper."

"Um, another time," Cole said, moving back until he bumped the counter. "Jamie, come meet Bella Nicholson."

Bella abruptly turned, her startled blue eyes finding Jamie's. "Hi." She smiled uneasily, glanced back at Cole, and then without hesitation met Jamie halfway.

They shook hands. "I'm Jamie Daniels."

Bella was a couple of inches taller, with gorgeous long blond hair that Jamie thought could win her quite a few commercials.

"You're not from around here," Bella said.

"Jamie's a guest at the Sundance." Cole put some money on the counter, and Abe tore his gaze away from the action long enough to hit a key on the ancient register.

"It's a dude ranch now," Sadie offered. "How many women you got out there, Cole, about fifteen?"

Bella's perfect eyebrows shot up. "A what?"

"It's not a dude ranch." Clearly disgusted, Cole muttered, "Jesus," under his breath. "We're still... Look, we have to go." He gestured impatiently for Jamie to precede him. "I'll call you at your folks' place, Bella."

"Sure." She seemed confused, a little unhappy, and Jamie wished she could just seep through the pine floorboards.

"Nice to meet you," Jamie and Bella said at the same time, and they both smiled.

Bella's lips had a wistful twist to them. Her gaze went to Cole. "I knew I'd end up blowing it with you," she said softly.

Cole noisily cleared his throat. "Good to have you back, Bella." He leaned toward her, hesitated, then gave her a brief kiss on the cheek.

"McAllister, you forgot your change." Abe leaned across the counter, obviously more interested in the minidrama than he was in the cash transaction.

Ignoring him, Cole hurried Jamie out the door. He didn't say anything, and she wasn't quite sure what to say either, as he walked her around to the passenger side of his truck.

After he opened the door for her, he settled his hat on his head and said, "We'll drive over to Marge's on the next block."

Jamie accepted his help climbing into the huge truck, then turned to him. "We don't have to stay."

She expected him to shut the door, wait until he got behind the wheel before continuing the conversation. But he stood right where he was, in the middle of Main Street, the door open.

"That wasn't what it looked like," he said, his gaze even with hers.

"It's okay," Jamie said. "You have a life here. I didn't think you were a monk, for goodness sakes."

"I want to explain. Bella and I—"

"You don't have to."

"Tough." He lifted her chin, leaned toward her, peering deep into her eyes. "Bella and I've known each other since junior high. We were off-and-on through high school. I'm two years older, and I left to give college a try. Then she graduated and didn't want to be tied to Blackfoot Falls. She comes back twice, maybe three times a year and we..." He shrugged. "We get together."

"Friends with benefits. I get it."

"I hate that damn term."

"Bella's right." Grinning, Jamie touched his cheek. "You are so cute."

A faint twitch at the left corner of his mouth was the closest thing to a smile she got. "I didn't want you to think I was one of those hound dogs sniffing at every skirt." He brushed his lips across hers. "I'm not that guy."

"I knew that without an explanation." Her breath caught when he slanted his mouth over hers and kissed her hard, for any and all of the good folks of Blackfoot Falls to see.

CLOTHES WERE GOING TO BE an issue, Jamie thought the next day as she rooted around in her duffel bag. She'd have to do a load of laundry, and she still had to talk to Rachel about staying an extra week. Although Jamie intended to spend every night with Cole, and despite the fact that everyone in the house probably knew it, she'd decided she wanted to have her own room.

Barbara McAllister seemed to like her, and Jamie wanted to keep it that way, not rub it in the woman's face that Jamie was having sex with her son. Cole had only mentioned an extra week, Jamie had to remind herself. There had been no talk of her coming back later, for the holidays or anything else. In fact, by the time they'd returned from town and Cole had done his evening chores, conversation had been minimal.

But when they had talked, really talked, it had been wonderful. She knew that he'd loved math and science in school, and he'd learned that she'd detested both subjects but had loved history and literature. They knew the names of the first boy and girl they'd kissed. He'd even told her about that day at the well and how he'd felt like a failure while everyone had labeled him a hero. In return, Jamie had confided feelings toward her parents she hadn't even shared with her friends, resentment she hadn't been aware of until he'd talked about his own family. He loved them completely and loved the Sundance. It made her a bit sad wondering if any woman could compete.

Cole had told her more about Bella, how everyone had expected that they'd get married until she left Blackfoot Falls for a more exciting life. He hadn't mentioned his own expectations, and Jamie hadn't asked. She had a feeling that his relationship with the blonde suited him perfectly. No-strings sex. And that bothered Jamie more than she cared to admit. Was she destined to become another Bella? Blowing into town a couple of times a year for some hot sex, and then *arrivederci?*

God, what was she doing getting ahead of herself? One extra week. That was it. She had her own life. A good life that she'd designed. How many women her age made the kind of money she did, answered to no one, traveled to their heart's content?

No more thinking. She had too much to do before Cole came to get her for their picnic dinner. Her friends expected her back tomorrow evening. She had to call them so they wouldn't send the National Guard after her. Then she had the car rental company to call, the airlines. Good God, she still had to write her blog. First though, she'd go find Rachel.

ON HIS WAY FROM the barn to the house, Cole saw the sheriff's truck coming up the drive. He'd seen Noah in town yesterday and Cole hoped this visit meant news of the stolen horse trailer.

He waited near the porch steps until Noah parked and walked toward him. As if reading his mind, Noah shook his head, his expression grim. "You got a few minutes?"

"Yeah, let's go in my office where it's cool."

Noah took off his hat and wiped his forehead with the back of his arm. "Wouldn't mind a glass of Hilda's lemonade."

"Looks as if you could use something stronger."

"I could, but I'll be on duty for a while yet."

"Well, damn, that doesn't sound good." It was close to dinnertime. Usually one of the deputies worked the second shift.

"Nope." Noah lowered his voice. "Another theft."

Cole stopped, his hand on the front door knob. "Who?"

"Avery this time. They took two of his saddles."

"What the hell is going on?"

"Wish I knew."

They entered the house, which was unusually quiet and empty, stopped briefly in the kitchen to grab some lemonade and then went into Cole's office off the den.

Cole sat behind his massive oak desk, and Noah took the old leather club chair. "Jesus, don't tell me you're here because Avery is pointing the finger at our guests again."

"You know him. Naturally he's shooting his mouth off." Noah shook his head. "Shit, had to be two of the orneriest old buzzards in the county…between him and Mrs. Clements, my phone hasn't stopped ringing for a week. All I need is for Gunderson to start in."

Cole sighed. After Mrs. Clements's four-wheeler had turned up, Cole had gone back to thinking Gunderson had taken the trailer. This new theft changed things—the McAllisters were no longer the only victims. "You got a culprit in mind?"

"We've had a couple of migrant workers come through town, but the timing's off. I'm not ruling anyone out."

"Yeah, we're not the only ranch circling the drain."

"You paid your boys yet?"

"About an hour ago." Cole knew where he was headed with this. "I heard some of them talking about going to Sadie's. I asked Josh and Kyle to keep their ears open."

"The Circle K guys have been paid. Two of them are already sitting at the bar. What about Rachel and Jamie? They going—"

"No." Cole saw the question in Noah's narrowed eyes. "I convinced Jamie to stay out of it. I'm counting on Rachel to have the good sense to do likewise."

Noah's concern changed to curiosity. "You serious about this Jamie woman?"

"What do you mean?"

Noah chuckled. "Buddy, I'm not sure how else to ask."

Cole smiled. "I like her."

"I knew that the first day she got here."

Cole rubbed the grit from the back of his neck, intent on a shower before his picnic with Jamie. "She's from L.A., so it's nothing long-term," he said, shrugging. He and Noah shared a lot, but this thing with Jamie… Talking about it didn't feel right. "She's a travel blogger. Rachel told me to give her some extra attention, make sure she has a good time so she'll give us a favorable review."

"That's all?"

"Yep."

"Bullshit."

"What?" Cole laughed. "You moonlighting for the *Gazette?*"

Noah flexed his shoulders, his grin fading. "Weeks like this, I'd rather have a job doing inventory for Abe." He checked his watch, then drained his lemonade and stood. "I hope something shakes loose tonight at Sadie's. Otherwise I'm afraid your trailer could be clear across the Canadian border by now."

JAMIE SAGGED AGAINST the wall outside of Cole's office, feeling so sick she feared she wouldn't make it upstairs. He was still talking to Noah, but she hadn't listened past the part about her. How could she have been such a fool?

She heard the back door open and close, and then Rachel's voice. Oh, God, Jamie had been looking for her…to see about keeping her room for another week. Biting down on her lip, she walked quickly and quietly to the stairs. She wanted to run all the way to her room, but why? There was no safety there. What she had to do was get out of this house, get away from the ranch. Get the hell out of Montana.

Once she'd reached the second floor, she heard Cole's and the sheriff's voices as they left the office. She made it to her room and started stuffing clothes into her duffel bag, her mind racing in a dozen different directions. If he knocked she wouldn't answer. He'd think she'd gone for a walk or was in the stable with Ginger or in the kitchen with Hilda or Rachel. With any luck he'd leave with Noah.

How in hell had she let this thing with Cole get so out of control? She'd never been into magical thinking or been a lovelorn sap. And yet she'd taken a week's worth of a vacation crush and turned it into the romance of the century.

It wasn't as if she didn't believe that Cole liked her. She'd be an idiot to think all that had been between them was faked for a good review, but all it added up to was great sex, a fun visit and a bittersweet goodbye.

It hit her as she stared at her stuffed duffel that it wasn't just Cole she'd gotten stupid about. It was the ranch, the family, the closeness and the safety. She'd been drawn in from the moment she'd set foot on their land. And Cole, well, Cole had been far more than just the icing on the cake.

Dammit, she should've known better. This kind of life was only a fantasy for her. She had no idea what it meant to belong to something permanent like the Sundance, to have a big family all around who would fight for each other and go to any lengths to keep the family and their land whole.

Her chest tightened and she had to blink hard to keep the tears at bay. She couldn't blame anyone for this mess but herself. Cole hadn't lied. He hadn't schemed. He'd felt the same attraction she had—she was certain of that. But he understood what the situation was. Temporary. Wanting to add another week was nice…it was great…but it wasn't a promise. Or a precursor or a test run. It was also impossible.

She'd give the Sundance five stars, talk it up on the blog, because they deserved it. The family was a joy; the ranch was an experience and a half for any city girl looking for something different. But she couldn't stay. Not when she'd let herself get so attached to a false hope. Her small carry-on was already in the bathroom. She opened it, and with a sweep of her hand she cleared the counter of her toiletries.

When she thought she heard footsteps she froze, holding her breath, listening until she was sure it was all right to move. She unplugged her laptop and cursed softly when she had to dump the contents of her purse onto the bed in order to find a piece of paper. She had to at least leave Rachel a note, explain there was an emergency back home and she had to hurry to the airport.

She gathered her things, then waited quietly by the door, her pulse speeding erratically as she turned for a final look at the bed where she and Cole had made love for the first time. No, what they'd had was sex, a brief encounter. She knew that now. And it hurt, the knifing pain in her heart and soul a mystery since she felt numb at the same time.

Damn her foolishness. She'd actually lain awake this morning thinking about how wonderful it would be to spend Christmas here with Cole, with the rest of the McAllisters. Barbara and Rachel weren't callous people who used others, they were just being nice. It made a horrible kind of sense that she'd attached herself to them like a leech, what with her friends all getting married. But finagling her way into a Montana ranch was not the solution. Even if her heart begged to differ. Cole… He was the rub. The way she felt about him was no fantasy. Under different circumstances, say he wasn't a rancher and she wasn't a travel blogger and they didn't live thousands of miles and a lifestyle away from each other…

Jamie briefly closed her eyes. No more magical thinking. What did she really know about these people? She had to leave. Get far away. Get back to her life. It was a good one, good enough, anyway.

She had a narrow window of time. Drinks would be served on the porch soon. Right now Rachel and Hilda would be busy in the kitchen. And Cole? God, she had no idea what she'd do if she ran into him. Not cry. No way. She'd never…

Inhaling deeply, she made sure she had a good grip on her things and headed for the stairs. Being loaded down with her bags and laptop made her descent tricky, but she managed to get to the porch unseen. A pair of wranglers working in the corral spotted her, but she kept her head down and walked straight to her rental car. Halfway there, Trace left the barn and saw her. But when he called out she quickened her pace, waved him off and shouted that she had an emergency.

It wasn't until she hit the main road that she let the tears flow.

SHOCKED AND NUMB, Cole stared at the note Rachel had handed him. Jamie was gone. Claimed she had an emergency. Scribbled on a piece of notebook paper she'd callously thrown on her dresser. He'd missed her by less than an hour.

"Did you talk to her at all?" he asked when he finally found his voice.

Rachel shook her head, her eyes full of concern and confusion. "I was in the kitchen when she left. I know that for a fact because Trace saw her get in her car."

"Did he talk to her?"

"No. She waved him off. He said she looked upset, which, if she had an emergency, makes sense. What I don't get is why she couldn't stop for thirty seconds to say something to me." Rachel worried her lower lip. "Did you guys have a fight?"

"'Course not. I came looking for our picnic supper, didn't I?" He sighed at the wounded look on his sister's face. "Sorry, I'm puzzled, is all." And he was starting to get angry.

Wasn't he worth a few minutes of her time? A phone call after she was on the road? How could she have left without so much as a goddamn goodbye? He'd thought…

What he'd thought was obviously wrong. The closeness he'd felt was wishful thinking. She'd been here for a vacation fling, and here he'd gone and convinced himself what they'd shared had been the beginning of something meaningful between them.

"We're jumping to conclusions here," Rachel said. "We don't know what the emergency is…. She could be pressed to catch a flight. I bet she calls when she gets to the airport."

"Yeah, you're right." He didn't believe it for a minute. He turned away and squinted out the kitchen window. He could hear the guests laughing and talking on the porch as they sipped their margaritas and beer and enjoyed Hilda's salsa and chips. Shit, he had to get out of here.

"If she doesn't, I'm sure I have her cell number…. Where are you going? What if Jamie calls?"

"Take a message. I have work to do."

"Cole, don't."

He let the screen door slam, then immediately veered left so he wouldn't have to force a smile for the women on the porch or, God forbid, have to stop and talk to them. He had nothing to say. To them, to Rachel, to anyone.

What the hell had happened? Shit, he couldn't even think clearly enough to replay their last hour together. Had he said something to spook her? Was it about Bella? No, couldn't be... Jamie had understood the situation. Though what the hell did he know about how she thought? Apparently, nothing.

What he did know for sure was that he had a missing horse trailer to worry about, the irrigation was still acting up and the auction in Missoula was just around the corner.

Her leaving was for the best, no question about it. He'd been neglecting his duties. Had she stayed, another week would've gone down the drain. Yeah, right now he felt like shit, but he'd get over it.

COLE CAUGHT A LOOSE STRAND of barbed wire with his hammer claw, then blinked furiously at the stinging sweat dripping into his eye. He carefully used the back of his shirt sleeve to blot his brow and forehead, then took the staple from his mouth. Before he could secure the strand, his thoughts skipped to Jamie. He lost his tentative hold of the wire, and swore. Repairing fence was his least favorite job and working alone was a bitch, but it also suited his foul mood to be miles from the ranch.

He couldn't afford to let his mind wander, not even for a second. Yet he'd sabotaged himself repeatedly in the week since she'd gone off without a word—smashed his thumb more than once. She hadn't called, and he'd been too stubborn to pick up the phone himself even though Rachel had made a point to give him Jamie's contact information. Why bother? Clearly she had nothing to say to him. Rachel had been oddly quiet, and he wondered if she'd spoken to Jamie, but he hadn't asked. And he hadn't visited Bella like he'd told himself a hundred times to do. The fact was, he had no interest in anyone but Jamie. Damn his stupidity.

"I brought you something to eat."

At the sound of Rachel's voice, he nearly jumped out of his boots. "What the hell are you thinking sneaking up on a man like that?"

Her brows raised, she glanced pointedly at the four-wheeler she'd driven, the one with the noisy engine. "You didn't eat breakfast, then skipped lunch, so here." She held out a wrapped sandwich. "I know you won't grab anything before the auction."

He peeled back his glove, exposing his watch. Christ almighty, how could he have forgotten about the auction? He barely had time for a shower. "Help me pick up these tools."

Rachel looked down at the mess he'd made. Various hammers and boxes of nails everywhere. He was usually more particular about tools and equipment. "You forgot, didn't you?" He refused to answer, and she added, "You can't go on like this. You've been foul-tempered and horrible. The boys try to avoid you, and Mom's worried. You have to call Jamie. Better yet, go see her."

Right. "What I gotta do is get to Missoula." He paused. "Have you talked to her?"

Rachel shook her head. "I've left two messages."

"Guess that's our answer." Cole picked up the tools, loaded his four-wheeler and drove like a maniac toward the ranch.

Within an hour he'd showered and was in his truck on his way to the auction. Jesse was going to kill him for being so late. His brother had taken one of the big trailers ahead early this morning, done some scouting.

The conversation with his sister kept circling in Cole's brain, mile after mile. Jamie wasn't the kind of person to run cold or ignore people. Something was very wrong, and he couldn't leave things this way. He needed to understand, needed to ask if he'd done something to push her away, needed to ask if he could've done or said something to make her stay.

Hell, he hadn't even told her how much he cared for her.

Cole checked the rearview mirror, saw that there were no cars coming, then swung a U-turn. He'd given his heart and soul to the ranch and his family, but part of the legacy of the Sundance was the love that had grown from generation to generation. Who was he to mess that up? Maybe Jamie wasn't the one, but he'd be damned if he wouldn't at least take the chance that she could be.

JAMIE STARED AT her laptop screen, sick to death of answering posts about the McAllister brothers. In spite of the tears she'd cried on her way home, regardless of the three pounds she'd gained from stuffing herself with chocolate ice cream in the week since she'd come back, she'd acted like a big girl and given the ranch the review it deserved.

Her only regret was that she'd been late posting the blog, really late, for the first time ever. Even when she'd returned from Bali, sick as a dog with the flu, she hadn't taken so long. So of course her regular readers were having a high time teasing her about having too much fun with the brothers and asking her which one she'd lassoed for herself. Rachel would see all of it.

Jamie needed a new line of work. Seriously. These women were making her crazy…something she could easily do by herself. She got offline and headed for the couch and the remote control. Her cell rang, and as much as she wanted to ignore it, she knew it was probably Linda or Kaylee, and if she didn't answer they'd be over in minutes to confiscate her Ben & Jerry's stash, and generally annoy the hell out of her. Then again, maybe it was Cole. Fat chance. No reason for him to call.

God, she missed him—his smile, his laugh, the way his eyes crinkled at the corners, the way he knew how to touch her… It was so crazy and totally unlike her. Did she have no pride?

She checked the caller ID, and mercifully it was only the dentist's office. She'd call them later. She plopped down on the couch, located the remote under a pile of tissue boxes and pillows and heard a knock at the door.

"Dammit." She rubbed her gritty eyes and forced herself to her feet. No use ignoring the knocking. Her friends had keys, which Jamie decided then and there she'd have to remedy.

She opened the door with a frustrated sigh, then reared back in total shock. "Cole?"

His hat in his hands, he looked up and steadily met her gaze. "Hi," he said, his mouth lifting in a tentative smile.

"What are you doing here?"

"I, uh… We need to talk."

"Oh. Uh, come in." She touched her ratty hair and winced. She hadn't even brushed it yet, or shaved her legs, or done anything to make herself human. Oh, crap.

He walked by her into the condo as she held the door. His jeans looked brand-new and his boots were as clean as she'd ever seen them. "Nice place," he said.

She rushed past him and picked up a pair of ice cream bowls, some discarded napkins and an empty pizza box left on the glass coffee table. Balancing everything in front of her to hide the hole in her oversize T-shirt and frayed cutoffs, she faced him. "If you can find a place to sit, be my guest."

He didn't move. "I've missed you."

Her breath caught, and she stared back, searching for the right words. "I have to get rid of these," she said, her voice cracking. "Want anything to drink while I'm in the kitchen?"

Cole took the pizza box from her and set it back on the table, along with his hat. Then he took her hands and lightly squeezed them. "I need to know why you ran off."

Jamie swallowed. She knew she hadn't misunderstood his

conversation with Noah, so then why was he here? "Aren't you supposed to be at some big important auction or something?"

"How am I supposed to pay attention to ranch business after the way you left? You had to know I'd be worried."

"Actually, no. I—I thought—" She took a deep shuddering breath. "I had a great time with you, Cole. Seriously great. But honestly, it was time for me to go. I was getting a little too attached to being at the Sundance…and, well…that wouldn't have done either of us any good. You have that great family. I don't even know what that feels like. This…" She pulled her hand away and helplessly waved at the sum total of her sorry life. "This is the closest thing to a permanent home I've ever had…. My apartment's a mess, I'm a mess…." Her voice cracked again. "It was the best vacation fling ever, honest. But what you need is to find yourself a nice ranch wife."

Cole smiled. "Wait a minute. Let me see if I've got this straight. You ran because you liked me? Liked the ranch and my family?"

She felt her face heat. Again. "It might have been a little more than just like."

Cole moved closer to her and made sure she met his gaze. "You're not the only one who was getting attached. I'm not sure it's time to pick out rings, but dammit, something was happening between us. If you're trying to tell me you don't want that, then fine, I'll go. But you should know right now, it wasn't ever just a vacation fling. Not for me." He reclaimed her hand, kissed the back, kept looking into her eyes.

"Oh. Oh, God."

"The way I feel about you, I've never felt about a woman before, Jamie. I don't even know how to describe it. Can't we give this thing a little more time? See how it shakes out?"

She laughed and sniffed at the same time. For Cole, that was incredibly romantic. What was more important than his words, as wonderful as they were, was that he was here. In her arms, in West L.A., California. He'd left his beloved ranch and he'd come to *her*. She wasn't crazy. He wanted more. More of her, with her L.A. life and her blog and all the other baggage she carried with her. "I'd like that," she said, her voice a little rocky because of the tightness in her throat.

He pulled her into his arms, and she slid hers around his neck. He kissed her long and hard, and then lifted his head. She blinked furiously, trying to quash the threat of tears.

"What's this?" he asked, his voice low and tender as he wiped her cheek. "Don't cry, sweetheart."

"I'm not."

He rubbed her back and gazed at her with such warmth she almost really did lose it. "My mistake," he whispered, bringing her close and tucking her under his chin.

She shook her head. "Oh, hell. Yes, I am. But they're happy tears."

"Well then, I reckon that's all right."

She heard the smile in his voice and she sighed, wondering how long he could stay. How long she could keep him tied to her bed. "Where are your things? You should bring them in."

He didn't answer. In fact, he got so quiet and still she leaned back, worried.

"I don't have anything but a razor and these new jeans and shirt I bought on the way."

"What do you mean? You didn't bring clothes?" Jamie's chest tightened. Was this it? He'd said what he had to say and now he was turning around?

"I was on my way to the auction…" He grinned crookedly. "Made a U-turn and headed south instead."

"You drove straight here all the way from Montana?" she asked, and he nodded. "What about the auction? Last week you said it was important…."

"Jesse's got it covered. He's been to plenty of auctions before. He knows what to do."

Jamie was stunned. He'd dropped everything to find her and give the two of them a chance. Holy… The tears were really going to start now. She swallowed hard, trying to hold back the flood.

"Jamie? Honey?" Cole said, and touched her cheek, his eyes full of concern.

She gave him a watery smile. "No one's ever skipped an auction for me before."

"Fools."

"You're probably exhausted."

He nodded. "I should go right to bed." Then he frowned. "Maybe after a shower."

The reality of Cole was starting to sink in. Not a dream, not a wish. He was the real thing, and what he was asking for was a lot. It would be complicated, what with her living in L.A. and him so far away. On the other hand, he'd just proved that distance didn't matter a damn when something was truly important. "I think we can arrange that," she said, "but first…"

His eyebrows rose and he leaned in just enough to let her know she was all his. "Yeah?"

"Kiss me, cowboy."

"Yes, ma'am," he said, and lifted her into his arms. "Yes, ma'am."

* * * * *

Can't wait to see more of the hot men around
Blackfoot Falls? Look for OWN THE NIGHT,
the next book in Debbi Rawlins's
MADE IN MONTANA *miniseries,*
coming out in October.

REQUEST YOUR FREE BOOKS!
2 FREE NOVELS PLUS 2 FREE GIFTS!

red-hot reads!

YES! Please send me 2 FREE Harlequin® Blaze™ novels and my 2 FREE gifts (gifts are worth about $10). After receiving them, if I don't wish to receive any more books, I can return the shipping statement marked "cancel." If I don't cancel, I will receive 6 brand-new novels every month and be billed just $4.49 per book in the U.S. or $4.96 per book in Canada. That's a saving of at least 14% off the cover price. It's quite a bargain. Shipping and handling is just 50¢ per book in the U.S. and 75¢ per book in Canada.* I understand that accepting the 2 free books and gifts places me under no obligation to buy anything. I can always return a shipment and cancel at any time. Even if I never buy another book, the two free books and gifts are mine to keep forever.

151/351 HDN FEQE

Name _____ (PLEASE PRINT)

Address _____ Apt. #

City _____ State/Prov. _____ Zip/Postal Code

Signature (if under 18, a parent or guardian must sign)

Mail to the **Reader Service:**
IN U.S.A.: P.O. Box 1867, Buffalo, NY 14240-1867
IN CANADA: P.O. Box 609, Fort Erie, Ontario L2A 5X3

Not valid for current subscribers to Harlequin Blaze books.

Want to try two free books from another line?
Call 1-800-873-8635 or visit www.ReaderService.com.

* Terms and prices subject to change without notice. Prices do not include applicable taxes. Sales tax applicable in N.Y. Canadian residents will be charged applicable taxes. Offer not valid in Quebec. This offer is limited to one order per household. All orders subject to credit approval. Credit or debit balances in a customer's account(s) may be offset by any other outstanding balance owed by or to the customer. Please allow 4 to 6 weeks for delivery. Offer available while quantities last.

Your Privacy—The Reader Service is committed to protecting your privacy. Our Privacy Policy is available online at www.ReaderService.com or upon request from the Reader Service.

We make a portion of our mailing list available to reputable third parties that offer products we believe may interest you. If you prefer that we not exchange your name with third parties, or if you wish to clarify or modify your communication preferences, please visit us at www.ReaderService.com/consumerchoice or write to us at Reader Service Preference Service, P.O. Box 9062, Buffalo, NY 14269. Include your complete name and address.

HB11B

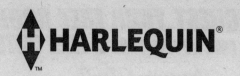

HARLEQUIN®

SYTYCW SO YOU THINK YOU CAN WRITE

Harlequin and Mills & Boon are joining forces in a global search for new authors.

In September 2012 we're launching our biggest contest yet—with the prize of being published by the world's leader in romance fiction!

Look for more information on our website, **www.soyouthinkyoucanwrite.com**

So you think you can write? Show us!

Enjoy this sneak peek of USA TODAY *bestselling author*
Maureen Child's newest title
UP CLOSE AND PERSONAL

Available September 2012 from Harlequin® Desire!

"**L**aura, I know you're in there!"

Ronan Connolly pounded on the bright blue front door, then paused to listen. Not a sound from inside the house, though he knew too well that Laura was in there. Hell, he could practically *feel* her standing just on the other side of the damned door.

He glanced at her car parked alongside the house, then glared again at the still-closed front door.

"You won't convince me you're not at home. Your car is parked in the street, Laura."

Her voice came then, muffled but clear. "It's a driveway in America, Ronan. You're not in Ireland, remember?"

"More's the pity." He scrubbed one hand across his face and rolled his eyes in frustration. If they were in Ireland right now, he'd have half the village of Dunley on his side and he'd bloody well get her to open the door.

"I heard that," she said.

Grinding his teeth together, he counted to ten. Then did it a second time. "Whatever the hell you want to call it, Laura, your car is *here* and so are you. Why not open the door and we can talk this out. Together. In private."

"I've got nothing to say to you."

He laughed shortly. That would be a first indeed, he told himself. A more opinionated woman he had never met. He had to admit, he had enjoyed verbally sparring with her. He admired a quick mind and a sharp tongue. He'd admired her even more once he'd gotten her into his bed.

He glanced down at the dozen red roses he held clutched in his right hand and called himself a damned fool for thinking this woman would be swayed by pretty flowers and a smooth speech. Hell, she hadn't even *seen* the flowers yet. At this rate, she never would.

Huffing out an impatient breath, he lowered his voice. "You know why I'm here. Let's get it done and have it over then."

There was a moment's pause, as if she were thinking about what he'd said. Then she spoke up again. "You can't have him."

"What?"

"You heard me."

Ronan narrowed his gaze fiercely on the door as if he could see through the panel to the woman beyond. "Aye, I heard you. Though, I don't believe it. I've come for what's mine, Laura, and I'm not leaving until I have it."

Will Ronan get what he's come for?

Find out in Maureen Child's new title
UP CLOSE AND PERSONAL

Available September 2012 from Harlequin® Desire!

HDEXP0912